Smith, Rosamond.

You can't catch me.

MAR 24 1995

$19.95

DATE			

YOU CAN'T CATCH ME

Rosamond Smith

YOU CAN'T CATCH ME

A WILLIAM ABRAHAMS BOOK

DUTTON

DUTTON
Published by the Penguin Group
Penguin Books USA Inc., 375 Hudson Street,
New York, New York 10014, U.S.A.
Penguin Books Ltd, 27 Wrights Lane,
London W8 5TZ, England
Penguin Books Australia Ltd, Ringwood,
Victoria, Australia
Penguin Books Canada Ltd, 10 Alcorn Avenue,
Toronto, Ontario, Canada M4V 3B2
Penguin Books (N.Z.) Ltd, 182–190 Wairau Road,
Auckland 10, New Zealand

Penguin Books Ltd, Registered Offices:
Harmondsworth, Middlesex, England

First published by Dutton, an imprint of Dutton Signet,
a division of Penguin Books USA Inc.
Distributed in Canada by McClelland & Stewart Inc.

First Printing, March, 1995
10 9 8 7 6 5 4 3 2 1

MAR 24 1995

Copyright © The Ontario Review, Inc., 1995

 REGISTERED TRADEMARK—MARCA REGISTRADA

Library of Congress Cataloging-in-Publication Data

Smith, Rosamond.
        You can't catch me / Rosamond Smith.
            p.   cm.
        "A William Abrahams book."
        ISBN 0-525-93947-4
        1. Middle aged men—United States—Psychology—Fiction.   2. Serial
    murders—United States—Fiction.   3. Identity (Psychology)—Fiction.
    4. Sexual deviation—Fiction.   I. Title.
    PS3565.A8Y5   1995
    813'.54—dc20   94-33475
                                                                    CIP

Printed in the United States of America
Set in New Baskerville
Designed by Leonard A. Telesca

PUBLISHER'S NOTE
This is a work of fiction. Names, characters, places, and incidents either are the products of the author's imagination or are used fictitiously, and any resemblance to actual persons, living or dead, events, or locales is entirely coincidental.

for Sallie and Jerry Goodman

I am another. . . .

—RIMBAUD

I

1 Tristram Heade's tragic adventure began inauspiciously, and surely by chance: as he was preparing to leave the train in Philadelphia, making his way along the narrow aisle of the Pullman car, a suitcase in one hand and a valise in the other, he felt someone tap his arm, and turned, and it was one of the black porters, who said, politely, "Sir, I believe you dropped your wallet—?" Taken by surprise, Tristram murmured his thanks, seeing, yes, the wallet was his, or so closely resembled his own as to be virtually identical with it: a wallet larger than most American wallets, measuring about six inches by four, but flat, in shape rather like a notebook; made of dark leather of no particular distinction, and fairly well-worn. He gripped his valise under one arm, and managed to slip the wallet into a convenient pocket of his coat; then moved on quickly, urged by his fellow passengers, who were crowding close behind him. The train from Richmond, Virginia, to Philadelphia, an overnight "express," was nearly two hours behind schedule, and tempers were short.

Out on the platform, however, Tristram regretted not having taken time to give the porter a tip. The man had been exceptionally kind after all. And Tristram did not know his name, and had not, to his shame, taken much notice of his face . . . except to know, and surely such knowledge was less than helpful, in the context of railroad porters, that the man was black; and that his expression had borne, beneath its courteous, even smiling surface, a look of bone-weary impatience with travelers like Tristram Heade, forever losing things, and dependent upon others for help. Over the course of years Tristram had several times lost his wallet, and various pieces of luggage; any number of pairs of gloves, hats, umbrellas; even, once, a rare, and very expensive, leatherbound first edition of Dickens's *Bleak House* which he had bought only a few hours before. And another time, years ago, on his first crossing to Europe, he'd absentmindedly left a thick wad of fifty-dollar bills in a lounge of the old S.S. *France*, which had not, of course, been there when he returned to look for it. . . .

"Mister? Are you waiting for a taxi?"

Tristram woke from his reverie to see a taxi idling a few yards away, the driver, a bushy-haired and -whiskered young man, already opening the rear door for Tristram to climb in. "Yes in fact I am," Tristram said belatedly. Again, he was taken by surprise; he'd made his way without thinking out of the crowded and rather disagreeably clamorous station to the taxi stand, trustingly following other suitcase-bearing men and women who had disembarked from the Richmond train. Though Tristram made the trip north to Philadelphia on the average of two or three times a year, and had done so for the past eleven years, primarily for the purpose of buying antiquarian books, he did not know the Philadelphia railroad station with any degree of confidence. And the task of getting a taxi, whether hailing one on the street, or waiting for one, as passengers did here, in an informal, jostling queue, always rather discountenanced him.

Yet: here was a taxi, as if by magic, and an obliging, smiling driver.

"Thank you very much," Tristram said, as the man took his suitcases from him, and stored them away in the trunk, "—but aren't these people ahead of me? There seems to be a line—"

"Nope, just get in, mister," the driver said, "—no problem."

"But don't you think—"

"Where to, mister?"

"—these others, who are waiting—"

"Nope. No problem."

So Tristram shrugged, and got into the cab, his leather valise gripped under his arm. It had not escaped his embarrassed notice that a number of men and women were staring at him, and at the taxi driver, with looks of resentment and curiosity; there were murmurings, exclamations —*Who the hell is that guy?* Indeed, it did not fail to strike Tristram as odd that he, so frequently ignored in situations of this kind, his natural good nature and passivity making of him a victim of others' self-assertion, should be singled out for preferential treatment, and by a total stranger; back home in Richmond, in, at least, the residential district in which he lived his bachelor's quiet life, and where the name Heade had a distinct old-aristocratic value, the solicitude of a taxi driver would have seemed more credible. But here in Philadelphia where no one knew him . . .

The driver was squinting at Tristram through his rearview mirror. "Where to, mister? Rittenhouse Square? —It was Rittenhouse Square last time."

"Last time?" Tristram asked.

"—you were in my cab."

Tristram didn't remember; but of course it was entirely possible. He said, "Yes, Rittenhouse Square, the Hotel Sussex on Rittenhouse Square."

And so the adventure began.

That in fact there was a beginning; a primary cause; a moment when things might have gone differently—that, given the laws of logic no less than those of human experience, there had to be such—Tristram Heade would not have doubted; but this would be retrospective knowledge. That spring evening in Philadelphia, he did not think of such things. Travel-weary, mildly disoriented from a long and rather rocky trip,—the railroads of this country have become unendurable, one of Tristram's fellow passengers complained, in the dining car—Tristram wanted now only to check into his hotel, bathe, telephone an elderly, invalid Heade uncle, with whom he hoped to dine later that week; and go down to dinner himself, as he always did, at the Sussex; and retire early for the night. And in the morning,—ah, the morning!—his spirits lifted at the prospect— he had an appointment with Virgil Lux, the antiquarian book dealer from whom, over the course of years, he had bought a number of precious books. He was quite excited about the prospect of acquiring, at last, no matter the cost, a rare quarto edition of . . .

As the taxi turned onto Rittenhouse Square, Tristram sat up suddenly, and said, "I've changed my mind: take me to the Hotel Moreau."

The driver squinted at him through the rearview mirror. "The Moreau?"

"Yes. I believe it's just on the opposite side of the Square."

How strange, Tristram thought. He knew nothing, or very little, about the Hotel Moreau; had never stayed there; nor had he, unless memory failed him, so much as dined there. Yet suddenly he felt a compulsion to be taken there; *and nowhere else.*

The Moreau, on the south side of the Square, was a smaller hotel than the Sussex; marble-fronted, with an elegant Egyptian-styled portico and tall spiky evergreens in enormous urns; a look of European comfort; an atmosphere even more subdued, yet even more aristocratic, than that of the Sussex. That it was even more expensive Tristram did not doubt; but what did *that* matter? It was a beautiful hotel. The thought had come to Tristram that it was urgent for him to surround himself with beauty, no matter the expense.

And he was so courteously, one might almost say royally treated, there: as soon as his taxi pulled up under the portico, a uniformed doorman stepped quickly forward, to help him out, and to take his bags inside. In the lobby, he had only to approach the desk and the chief clerk stood at attention, and smiled; and the hotel manager himself appeared, smiling, very nearly bowing, murmuring, "Ah! This is unexpected, Mr. Markham! But I am sure we can accommodate you."

Tristram stopped in his tracks, and stared, and said, "Did you say 'Markham'? My name is not Markham, but Heade. Tristram Heade."

"I assume you would like your usual suite, Mr. Markham?"

"My name is not 'Markham,' but 'Heade.' 'Tristram Heade.' "

The manager continued to smile; fixing Tristram with a rather sharp, inquisitive look. He was a small, slender, foxfaced man with a minute waxy moustache. "As you like, sir. There is no trouble about that, sir."

"I'm afraid I didn't make a reservation," Tristram said apologetically. "I only now arrived in the city, and—"

"No trouble about that, sir. I am sure we can accommodate you, sir, and with your usual suite."

"I don't believe, though," Tristram said, frowning, "that I have a 'usual' suite here. I usually stay across the Square, in fact, at the—"

"Of course, sir, whatever you say, sir," the manager murmured, with, now, a small subtle smile, "but I'm sure we can accommodate you, in any case. Will you give me two or three minutes to make arrangements?"

"If it's the slightest bit of trouble, please don't—"

"*No* trouble, sir, I assure you," the dapper little man said.

There followed then a whispered consultation between the manager and the desk clerk, during which Tristram had the uneasy impression that the Hotel Moreau was indeed filled; or would shortly be filled; and that special measures were being taken on his account. Several times he was about to say that it really did not matter—since he had a reservation at the Sussex he could simply go there. But the lobby of the Moreau with its crystal chandeliers, its rich furnish-

ings and decorations, its atmosphere of studied, under-
stated, yet seductive old-world charm, so pleased his eye,
and awakened in him a dim, yet disturbingly powerful memory of the kind we feel for dreams lost upon waking, he said
not a word. He thought, If I am here, they must rearrange
things for me. For after all they would not wish to offend
me.

And so Tristram Heade was given a room; a suite of
rooms; on the very top floor. As Tristram was signing his
name—in his large childlike hand, in which each letter was
plainly displayed: *Tristram Joseph Heade*—the manager stood
at his elbow, murmuring, with a small mysterious smile, "I
hope the Louis Quatorze suite will prove as satisfactory as it
has in the past, Mr. Mar—, I mean Mr. Heade, but if there
is anything you should like, or any complaint you might
have, please do not, of course, hesitate to call the desk. I
assure you, I will personally do all I can, to make your stay
at the Moreau pleasant."

"I should hope so," Tristram said, with a quiet laugh.
"For, after all . . ." But his words trailed off since he did
not know quite what he meant to say, or even what he
meant. His face warmed in embarrassment. He was the sort
of man, a gentlemanly man, an oldish young man, at the
age of thirty-five rather boyishly middle-aged, as, at the age
of twelve, he had seemed prematurely adult, who shrinks
from special favors and privileges; as the last-living scion of
an old, once distinguished, now moribund Virginia family,
he was both embarrassed and annoyed by flattery; though
surrounded in his younger life by family servants, he had
never so much as given an order to them, or raised his voice
in self-assertion. For it was a matter of pride, in a sense; a
prideful sort of humility. A true gentleman, Tristram's
grandfather once told him, never presumes upon his own
position in the world.

Now Tristram murmured conciliatory words, and shook
the manager's hand, thanking him for his kindness.

"I assure you, Mr. Markham," the man said, with a quite
dazzling smile, "—it is *our* pleasure."

Tristram raised a forefinger as if in warning. " 'Heade,' you know. 'Tristram Heade.' "

"Of course, sir. No trouble at all, sir. 'Tristram Heade.' "

In the Louis Quatorze suite, which was, indeed, a lavish, beautifully appointed set of rooms, with a striking view of the leafy Square and of tree-lined streets of brownstone houses to the south, Tristram strolled about in a sort of daze, thinking, They are mistaking me for someone else . . . and what a wide, deep swath this "someone else" cuts in the world!

If he had heard correctly, the other's name was Markham. It was a pity he had not been cagey enough to determine the first name.

2 Before dinner, Tristram bathed in the luxurious black-marble tub in the bathroom, and shaved for the second time that day, wondering at the silvery-blond stubble on his cheeks and chin; his beard usually grew at a far slower rate. He regarded his reflection rather shyly in the ornamental mirror, and could not have said whether he was (as his late mother, and numerous of his female Heade relatives, insisted) an unusually attractive man; or whether he was a man whose features, impressive in themselves, did not quite fit together, like a puzzle whose parts had loosened.

His skin was fair, and thin; his hair so pale a blond as to appear nearly white, like an albino's; his eyebrows and lashes were white as well, and his eyes, round, childlike, intelligent, so faint a blue as to seem colorless, like washed glass. He was nearsighted, and had been so since childhood; when daylight began to fade, his astigmatism became more pronounced. He wore wire-rimmed glasses whose frames, unchanged for fifteen years, fitted his face tightly. The bones of his face were strong, even blunt, but his habitual expression was one of patience, passivity, and, to a degree surprising in so masculine a figure, sweetness; there was something soft, or softened, about him; as if an abrupt movement or a rude word might cause him distress. Tristram *feels* so very strongly, his mother had said of him, when he was a boy. He had not known at the time, nor did he know now, whether the statement was affectionate, or worried; boastful, or censorious. Nor did he even know if it was true.

He was in any case a large man, standing just above six feet four inches tall, and weighing two hundred twenty pounds; there was nothing dainty, or graceful, about him. Since late adolescence he had had a bearish figure, with his short-trimmed whitish hair, and fair flushed skin, and white-lashed eyes, and an ambling, rather rolling gait. It was his custom to have his hair cut very short, and allow it to grow out, so that, immersed in his bachelor's routine in Richmond, he need not trouble with it for weeks; before leaving he had gone to his barber, and, to his vague embarrassment, now sported a haircut so short as to resemble a brush cut; which exposed his large pinkish-translucent ears, and ungainly ears he thought them, in which, to his annoyance, stiff white hairs grew. . . . If I am a bear, Tristram thought, I am a polar bear: an albino.

It seemed to him preposterous, suddenly, that another man might be mistaken for him. With his many flaws, surely Tristram Heade was sui generis?

Though self-conscious about dining alone in public, and armed with a book (a first edition, 1870, of Charles Dickens's last, unfinished novel *The Mystery of Edwin Drood*, carefully wrapped in plastic), Tristram had little difficulty that evening: simply to enter the Fountain Room of the Hotel Moreau with its innumerable gilded mirrors and flickering candlelight and vases of fragrant waxy-white roses on the tables was to incur the respectful attention of the maitre d', and the head waiter, and the wine steward, and a small platoon of waiters and busboys who were, throughout his two-hour meal, uniquely solicitous of him. (And were there not quizzical, admiring glances from other diners?—including elegantly dressed, bejeweled women?) Tristram had never been a person to fuss over food, and was as far from a gourmet diner as one might be; truly, he cared little what he ate, so long as it was nourishing and good. How odd then that, tonight, he ate and drank with a zestful appetite— appetizers of steak tartar and scallops seviche, an entree of lobster Newburgh, dishes he'd never before found remotely tempting—and an entire bottle of a tart, delicious 1963 French Chardonnay. And he forgot entirely about opening *Edwin Drood.*

And where in the past the protocol of tipping had always embarrassed him, suggesting as it does that one is superior to another, tonight Tristram had no scruples about tipping very generously indeed. "Thank you, Mr. M— Mr. *Heade*," the maitre d' said, smiling and bowing as Tristram left. "Always a pleasure, sir!"

When, at midnight, Tristram returned to his luxurious suite, it was to discover to his surprise a bottle of chilled champagne awaiting him; a tall vase of those waxy-white roses; a sumptuous cornucopia of fruits, bonbons, chocolates, and several tiny bottles of brandy, with the accompanying handwritten card: *Mr. Angus Markham—compliments of the house.*

What to do?—telephone the front desk immediately, and demand to speak to the manager? Or wait until morning? Tristram absentmindedly chewed a bonbon or two, and uncorked a bottle of Benedictine brandy. Perhaps I am making too much of this, he thought. Perhaps "Mr. Angus Markham" would find it all amusing.

So he went to bed, and slept well; far more soundly than he'd ever slept in the Hotel Sussex; not waking, to his shame, until nearly nine o'clock the next morning . . . a good two hours past his usual time for getting up. Yet he felt wonderfully rested; refreshed; with a good appetite for breakfast; and a sense of excited elation about the day to come. His eleven o'clock appointment with Mr. Lux was foremost in his mind: he had been anticipating their meeting for weeks. Mr. Lux was allowing Tristram to see, before any of his other customers, a rare quarto edition of . . .

Suddenly, while dressing, he discovered to his amazement an extra suitcase in his room; a handsome leather suitcase of about the size, and the quality, of his own, though it was much newer than his, and free of the various scuff-marks, scratches, and labels affixed to his own. Where had this come from? Had the taxi driver absentmindedly taken another man's suitcase, at the station, and put it into his trunk?

He checked the closet, and discovered that someone had hung up a stranger's clothes mixed with his own; it must have been the chambermaid, the evening before, while he'd been at dinner. There were several coats, shirts, pairs of impeccably creased trousers . . . even, arranged on the floor, several pairs of shoes of about the size, though not the style, of Tristram's own shoes. "This is terrible," Tristram said aloud, staring into the closet. He had, once,—had it been in Philadelphia, in fact? many years ago?—lost a suitcase of his own, and remembered how desperate he'd felt.

Unfortunately, there was no identification label on the suitcase. He could see where it had been attached to the handle, but had been torn off.

Looking through his own things Tristram found, again to his amazement, a wallet, a stranger's wallet, in one of the pockets of his herringbone suit coat; the coat he'd worn yesterday on the train. The wallet resembled his own yet was not his own, for his remained where he'd laid it the night before, on top of the bedroom bureau. In a moment all became clear, or nearly: the porter had handed Tristram the wrong wallet, and in the confusion of the moment, too timid to wish to annoy his fellow passengers, Tristram had accepted it without question. "So I myself am the cause of all this," he said aloud. "I am to blame."

Placed side by side, the wallets differed significantly. Though of approximately the size and dimensions of Tristram's wallet, the stranger's wallet was made of a rich hand-tooled kidskin, while Tristram's was ordinary leather; it was so new as to smell, still, of newness, while Tristram's, a Christmas gift from his mother, dead now for years, was frayed and worn smooth from constant handling. It did not surprise Tristram, though it dismayed him, that the stranger's wallet had been emptied of cash and credit cards; even of change; in fact it contained nothing but an identification card, partly torn, with only the typed name ANGUS T. MARKHAM remaining. No address! No telephone number!

"So, it is his," Tristram said, frowning. "And the other things too . . . I suppose."

He searched the wallet methodically, and found, in one of its compartments, a two-by-three-inch black-and-white photograph, very likely a passport photograph; which seemed to him, in the first flush of discovery, to have solved the mystery. For the man in the photograph resembled Tristram Heade, at least superficially . . . around the eyes, in particular, though he wore no glasses; and the mouth; and his hair, though more stylishly cut than Tristram's, appeared too to be very blond. He was of indeterminate age, anywhere between thirty and forty-five; leaner-jawed than Tristram; with none of Tristram's air of self-doubt; a man who knows his own worth, and will not be sold short. Tristram thought him, grudgingly, a handsome man; a ladies' man, by the look of him. He felt a mild stirring of revulsion.

Still, everything fell into place; or nearly. It was clear that Tristram resembled Angus Markham closely enough to have been mistaken for him by the Pullman porter (who must have checked the wallet, and come upon the photograph); and, coincidentally, by the taxi driver (who had, to Tristram's embarrassment, seemed to expect a more generous tip than Tristram had pressed into his hand: though that tip, by Tristram's standards, *had* been generous). As for the management of the Hotel Moreau . . . he would have to set them straight, or move out at once.

At any rate, Tristram thought, it has turned out to be a simple misunderstanding. He would make a telephone call or two to the proper authorities at the Philadelphia train station; and get Angus Markham's things returned to him as quickly as possible. He would speak with the manager of the hotel. He only hoped that, furious as he probably was, Angus T. Markham would not blame *him*.

3 So Tristram ordered breakfast from room service, and, while he ate, or tried to eat, made a half-dozen futile calls to the train station. It took him three calls simply to be put in contact with the party who might have been of assistance; but this person, after a lengthy search, during which time Tristram had no choice but to continue to press the receiver to his ear, and eat, in a desultory fashion, his cooling food, informed him that no one named "Angus T. Markham" was registered as having traveled on that particular train; there was no one named "Angus T. Markham" in the computer, dating back to 1981. Another call, equally frustrating, to the Lost and Found Office of the station, connected him with a person, whether male or female Tristram could not determine, who informed him, in a maddeningly indifferent voice, that, as of that morning, no one named "Angus T. Markham" had reported anything missing. "Wait," Tristram said quickly, as the clerk was about to hang up, "—could you look again? He *must* have filed a claim. I have his things here in my room as proof, if proof be required," Tristram said, not quite knowing what he said, "of the man's existence."

There followed then a long wait, while the clerk checked another time, or pretended to do so: without success. "Sorry, mister. No 'Angus T. Markham.'" Tristram said anxiously, "How is it possible that a passenger might lose his wallet and luggage, and not trouble to report it?" "Oh, people lose things on our trains all the time," the clerk said blandly, "and no one ever hears of them again." "The things, or the people?" Tristram asked. The clerk chuckled, as if that were the proper answer to Tristram's question; and asked him to leave his name and telephone number, in case "Markham" did come in. So Tristram did so, and hung up. It astonished him to see that he had spent two hours on the telephone . . . and that his scrambled eggs and Canadian bacon, long abandoned, had congealed in an unappetizing mess on his plate. The coffee pot, so hot at first that Tristram's fingertips were burned brushing against it, was now stone cold.

He telephoned Virgil Lux to apologize, and reschedule their appointment for early afternoon; dressed hurriedly; and, on his way out of the hotel, stopped at the front desk to explain, or to attempt to explain, that he was not, as the hotel management seemed to think, Angus T. Markham— "I am Tristram J. Heade, just as I am registered." None of the morning clerks seemed to know Tristram, however, and the manager had not yet come in. The head clerk checked the registration for the Louis Quatorze suite, and said, politely, "You are 'Tristram Joseph Heade, of Richmond, Virginia.' Is that not correct?" "That is correct," Tristram said, blushing, "but there seems to be a misunderstanding about my being 'Markham.' " Tristram knew himself regarded with curious, if resolutely polite stares. He said half-pleadingly, "Well—if a 'Mr. Markham' calls me, please tell him that his suitcase and things are in my room, and that I will be back in a few hours. If he likes, he is welcome to come over, and take them from my room, in my absence." "And who is 'Mr. Markham' again?—I'm afraid it isn't clear," the clerk said. "A man you say has taken your wallet and luggage by mistake, from your room?" "No, not at all," Tristram said irritably. "The reverse. Or, nearly the reverse." He checked his watch; it was nearly one o'clock. "I'll explain later," he said. "I'm afraid I don't have time now."

So, his face burning, he left the hotel; crossed Rittenhouse Square; and set out on his usual brisk pace in the direction of Twenty-second Street, a mile or so away, where, in a charming little mews called Chancellor Street, Lux's Rare Books & Coins, Est. 1889 had its shop. The April morning was warm and humid, the air in the streets touched with a faint garbagey odor; not in itself unpleasant, but less fresh than he might have wished. It was Tristram's custom to walk a good five or six miles every day, except in the most inhospitable weather. He knew Richmond so well he might have walked it blindfolded, but Philadelphia remained an unknown quantity, never to be mastered. Even the Rittenhouse Square district, which he had visited countless times, and happily tramped about in, was largely mysterious to him still . . . and the character of streets and neighborhoods seemed continually to be changing from one visit to the next.

This morning, however, he paid very little attention to his surroundings. The vexing problem of "Angus Markham,"—or was it the problem of "Markham/Heade"—occupied his thoughts. How peculiar it all was, and how . . . disturbing. Surely he was not to be held to account for stealing Markham's money? Markham's things? He knew himself guiltless; or, if guilty, guilty of nothing more than a moment's carelessness on the train. If only he had taken time to examine the damned wallet, he thought miserably, all this might have been avoided.

He tried to recall his fellow passengers on the train. He'd had two meals in the dining car, but had not encountered anyone who might be said to resemble him. He'd traveled by Pullman, as he always did; had slept poorly, as always; and had, as always, spent most of his time reading. Since boyhood, but particularly since the death of his parents, Tristram had been susceptible to fugues of daydreaming and forgetfulness; reverie-states in which his normal waking consciousness seemed to be suspended, and another, pleasurable, mysterious, oddly comforting, claimed authority. He rarely remembered what he dreamt of at such times except to understand that, lost in the labyrinthine passages of his own thoughts, he was neither awake nor asleep; and quite oblivious to the existence of the outside world. . . . His mother once said of him, Tristram *dreams* so very strongly.

Tristram's father had died when Tristram was twenty-three years old, and in his second year of law school at the University of Virginia; his mother had died when he was twenty-eight years old, and already, despite a modicum of success, as a young lawyer with one of the most distinguished of Richmond firms, disillusioned with his profession. He had never felt confident that he had been hired by the firm, for one thing, on his own merits—if, indeed, he had any merits; he was convinced it had been for his family name. He surely had little lawyerly talent, or cunning, of his own. To go for another's throat, however obliquely, by way of a staggeringly intricate system of language, and all of it fortressed by the rectitude of "the law"—did not appeal to him in the slightest.

So, following his mother's death, Tristram had simply resigned his position with the firm. And began to live a life of solitude, and utter contentment, in his parents' house; or, more precisely, in two or three rooms of his parents' twenty-room house; vaguely hoping that, yet, he *might* marry, as the Heades had quite naturally wanted him to do . . . but the years passed, and continued, almost dreamily, to pass . . . and he remained single; with his books, and walks, and the company now and then of a very few friends, bachelors like himself, shabbily well-to-do heirs of Virginia families once vigorous, ambitious, and aggressive. He ordered most of his books through the mail, knowing that the dealers with whom he did business could be trusted; and went out several times a year for what he thought of, in his quiet way, as "the adventure of newness," to antiquarian conferences, and to antiquarian shops in Philadelphia, Washington, and New York City. (Tristram had not, however, visited New York City for some time. Its very atmosphere, highly charged, yet inchoate, with so great a flood of stimuli on every side, had become worrisome to him.)

Taking the train out of Richmond was in itself an adventure; one never knows, after all, with whom one will sit in the dining car; or what casual, wayward, yet sometimes richly rewarding conversations one might strike up with total strangers. This past trip, Tristram had become acquainted with two elderly women who had known his mother's grandmother; with a numismatician on his way to a numismatics conference in Philadelphia; and with several children. (He was a man very fond of children so long as he was in their company. Apart from them, and apart from the idea of them, he never thought of them at all.) He'd exchanged friendly greetings with the train porters as always and only regretted that the porter who had given him Markham's wallet had not seemed to know his name. How easily the mix-up might have been avoided . . .

Suddenly he remembered having opened the door of the compartment beside his, absentmindedly; and glimpsing, inside, a man sitting in the near-dark (it was just dusk), evidently looking out the window, a drink in his hand. Tristram of course apologized immediately, and backed out; retaining only the impression that the stranger did not seem much startled or annoyed by the intrusion, and murmured something that sounded like, "Quite all right." And the next morning, making his way from one car to another, as the open air whistled about his head, and the floor swayed and lurched, Tristram collided with a man who, like himself, was having trouble keeping his balance; a stranger whose face he did not see clearly, except to remark, with the fleeting accuracy of perception we experience in such situations, that here was a face that seemed in some way familiar or significant . . . but the moment was fleeting. The two men bumped shoulders, murmured mutual apologies, and kept going. There was nothing more to it than that.

Now, however, Tristram wondered if the man in the compartment and the man with whom he had collided were the same man; and if that man was the elusive Angus T. Markham. For someone, after all, had to be Angus T. Markham.

. . . He rubbed his shoulder ruefully; it *did* hurt, and was probably bruised.

Tristram looked up to find himself on a traffic-congested corner; the intersection of Twenty-sixth Street and Charity, a street of which he had never heard. He had no idea whether Chancellor might be to his left or his right and saw, to his annoyance, that he was already ten minutes late for his appointment with Mr. Lux. The thought passed violently through his head that he was making too much of the Markham business, as he made too much of most things. And that it was very naive of him to care in the slightest whether a stranger's things were returned to him, so long as his own plans were not interrupted. Do you imagine, an interior voice lightly mocked, Markham would care in the slightest about *you?*

4 Tristram was relieved to see that Chancellor Street, which was scarcely more than an alley, had not much changed its old-world character; though Twenty-second and -third streets, which bounded it, had grown unpleasantly busy. Not only cars, taxis, and buses streamed past, but bicyclists as well, hurtling themselves forward without much concern for traffic lights or pedestrians.

Though Tristram had been looking forward to his appointment with Virgil Lux for weeks, he felt a stab of disappointment as soon as he stepped into the shop and heard the bell tinkle overhead. Why was he *here?*—why, of all places in Philadelphia, let alone the world, *here?* The place seemed to him distinctly dustier and shabbier than he remembered; with a sharp smell of mice; so jammed with old furniture and books that one could scarcely draw a deep breath. When Lux greeted him, and shook his hand, Tristram saw to his embarrassment that the older man was wearing a toupee; and that this toupee, youthful as it was, and of what appeared to be good quality, nonetheless made him look older than his age of sixty-five or thereabouts. Also, his wide, rather fawning smile revealed obvious false teeth. And one of his eyes had a vague milky cast, very like that of a dog owned, decades ago, by a black yardman who had worked for Tristram's father. . . . He wondered why he had not noticed these details before when now they struck his eye so jarringly.

Though Tristram was the soul of patience, so slowly and ponderously did Virgil Lux speak, describing the material he hoped his customer would buy, that Tristram soon grew restless; his mind began to wander. Shapeless as smoke, and as seemingly idle, his thoughts drifted free . . . and fixed upon, of all things, a female figure . . . a voluptuous, near-naked, faceless female figure. Tristram saw himself take the woman boldly in his arms; saw himself kiss her; felt her warm, eager lips; and her arms tight, strong, even convulsive, around his neck. His heart beat hard; blood rushed into his face. Who was this woman? Who in fact was this man?—for it could scarcely be Tristram Heade, so shamelessly impassioned.

"And here, Mr. Heade, you see . . . the initials presumed to be those of Her Majesty Queen Anne; and the date . . . though the ink is badly faded . . . 1709."

Tristram shifted uncomfortably in his seat, and made an effort to listen to Lux's words. The dealer had laid out on his counter an early eighteenth-century quarto edition of *The Tragedy of Macbeth, by Wm. Shakespeare*, a rare document, its aged leather binding intricately engraved; its fine print faded, but still legible. The item was listed in Lux's catalogue as "out of the personal library of Anne, Queen of England (1702–14)." When Tristram stared, and failed to respond, Lux said, apologetically, yet with an air of subtle resentment, that, since Tristram's last visit to Philadelphia, he had become "somewhat handicapped": he'd had a mild stroke, which was why, if Tristram wondered, his speech was slurred and his left hand partly paralyzed. Tristram said quickly, "I hadn't noticed." Then, because this sounded wrong, "—I'm very sorry to hear it." "Well," said Lux, sighing, "I am much recovered. Thank you."

As Lux continued with his slow, dogged presentation, and Tristram prepared, listlessly, to make his purchase—he had come, after all, so many hundreds of miles: he could not return empty-handed—another customer entered the shop; the bell tinkled another time. This customer was younger than Tristram by at least a decade, and had the boyish, pale, hungry look of a student besotted by books. He had come to browse, not to buy, for Lux's prices were too high for him, and, within minutes—it must have been a consequence of the dreary slanted dust-heavy light—he looked older; stooped over a bin of old books, his shoulders rounded, his face pinched, his skin a whitish cheesy texture. Old books, old bindings, old paper, old things . . . Tristram stared at the boy with something like horror.

Mr. Lux had asked him a question, but Tristram had not heard. It was time, he supposed, for him to take out his checkbook . . . to make his purchase. He glanced at his watch, however, and saw, alarmed, that most of the after-noon had drained away: it was nearly four-thirty!

He said, "The quarto is impressive, Mr. Lux, if it's genuine; but how do I know if it's genuine? I have only your word to go by."

For a long moment the old man simply stared at him. A complex scrim of emotions showed in his face—shock, hurt, apprehension, guilt. His milky eye had grown milkier.

He has been cheating me for years, Tristram thought.

Lux stammered, "Why, Mr. Heade, I . . . I scarcely know how to . . . to respond to such . . . a . . ."

Tristram was on his feet now, towering over him. He said politely, "I think I'll wait a while before deciding, Mr. Lux, if you don't mind. The quarto is rather expensive after all."

Still, Tristram did not want to embarrass Virgil Lux in front of another customer; so they parted amicably enough, with another handshake, this time rather forced, and Tris-tram's murmured promise that he would let Lux know his decision soon; by the end of the week, certainly. "I can't promise, Mr. Heade . . . that the quarto will still . . . be available," Lux said in a brave, feeble voice; and Tristram countered cheerfully, "That, then, is a risk I must take. As Macbeth advises us, 'If it were done when 'tis done, then 'twere well it were done quickly.' " He felt surprisingly little rancor; though he did not feel much pity either, or sym-pathy. And how light, how airy, how good it was, to feel, for once in his life, neither pity nor sympathy for another hu-man being. . . .

For, after all, a man in his position, so naive, so damnably trusting, with too much money and too little common sense, deserves to be bilked.

Out in the mews, where the hazy spring air had turned refreshingly sharp, Tristram drew a deep breath, and laughed aloud, in gratitude for his narrow escape.

He left Chancellor Street, and crossed Twenty-second, walking, now, briskly, though with no clear destination in mind. He suspected that Markham's things were still in his hotel room; and if they were, very well, then, they were; he did not intend to trouble himself any further. "You have tried hard enough to locate him. Your time is too precious to waste. Wear the things that fit you, and discard the rest." This admonition formed itself perfectly in his brain and he smiled with pleasure, as if he had thought of it himself.

5

"And what is this? *Is* it . . . an eye?"

Tristram turned the object in his fingers, staring. On the sidewalk it had looked like a child's marble but it was in fact, so very improbably, an eye: a glass eye. Tristram had stooped to pick it up while strolling on a tree-lined street in a neighborhood not known to him, of old, distinguished brownstone houses, his attention drawn to something gleaming amid a small pile of leaves. Since leaving Lux's shop, and walking for hours, briskly, exuberantly, he had found himself, with unusual appetite, *looking* at things; *observing* things; and thoroughly enjoying the experience. To be so acutely aware of his surroundings, so almost, one might say, aggressively alert, was not in Tristram Heade's natural character, and he almost feared he would relinquish the impulse once he returned to Richmond.

How strange! How very . . . strange! He turned the glass eye in his fingers, staring. He had never seen anything like it in his life. Not an eyeball as one might imagine it, but an artfully flattened sphere; the white not purely white, but subtly tinted, like a real human eye; the iris a tawny-brown-blue, absolutely convincing. And how particularly uncanny, to hold the thing in the palm of one's hand . . . for a long moment Tristram stood transfixed.

Tristram thought it a beautiful object, very like a precious jewel; yet rather terrifying. To contemplate a human eye, even an artificial eye, out of its socket, unprotected and un-contained by the eyelid, was a very odd, discomforting experience. He suppressed a shudder. Who had lost it, or discarded it, and why *here*, of all places? Whose had it been? Or had it never been fitted to any eyeless socket, never put to use? He seemed to know that, being glass, and thus predating 1930, it could not be a recently made eye; for glass eyes *per se* are no longer crafted. Though people refer to them as "glass" instead of . . . whatever in fact they are.

In any case, he would keep it. Of course. It was a good-luck talisman, surely; and not an omen of evil to come.

6 At the Hotel Moreau, when Tristram unlocked the door to his suite, it was to discover a fresh vase of white roses awaiting him—"compliments of the management"— and a selection of cocktail nuts; and, in his bedroom, atop his bureau, a handsome leather valise, not his (his was on the floor close by) though of a size and shape resembling his. There was no tag attached to the handle but there were gold-plated initials on the side—*A T M*. He checked the closet: no new clothes had been added, but, on the shelf, in prominent view, was a smart black bowler hat and, beside it, an ebony-black cane with an ornate carved handle.

This time, Tristram felt rather more resigned than annoyed; even, in a way, gratified; for, clearly, none of this was his fault . . . it could safely be said that he was as much a victim of the confusion as Markham, and could not possibly be blamed for the stupidity of others. He opened the valise, thinking, Whatever is inside is my due.

The valise, which smelled pungently of newness, contained only papers, several packets of letters, printed matter of various sorts, and a jacketless hardcover book—a well-worn copy of *The Rubaiyat* of Omar Khayyám. This *Rubaiyat* was no collector's item, Tristram saw, disappointed; just a mass-produced copy of the popular Edward Fitzgerald translation. He opened it at random, to these lines, underscored in pencil:

> I sent my Soul through the Invisible,
> Some letter of that After-life to spell:

And after many days my Soul return'd,
And said, "Behold, Myself am Heav'n and Hell."

(In Tristram's library in Richmond was an illustrated 1879
edition of Fitzgerald's translation, carefully kept in its original wrappers, and very nearly in mint condition, still. Tristram had been led to believe by the dealer from whom he
had bought the book,—in fact, it was Virgil Lux—that its
value would quadruple within a few years.)

There were dozens of real estate brochures in the valise,
with a concentration, it seemed, in Florida; in the Tampa-
Sarasota area and the Keys. Also, racetrack sheets from Florida, New York, and New Jersey. Also, several untidy packets
of letters, each held together with a rubber band. A com-
mingling of perfumes, sadly stale, lifted from the letters as
Tristram examined them. They had been written by women,
clearly, each in a distinctive feminine hand, and in a differ-
ing shade of ink. One ink was lavender, on stiff white stationery; another was a royal blue, on pale blue stationery;
still another deep crimson, on pale pink stationery. Though
his curiosity was whetted Tristram resolved not to read the
letters,—he was, he hoped, still that much of a Virginia
gentleman—but he could not help but notice that the first
letter of each packet was marked with a large penciled X.
And what does this mean? Tristram wondered. Account
closed?

Some of the real estate materials were underlined and
annotated; here and there, prices for properties were
crossed out and other, lower prices recorded in their places.
(The prices quite stunned Tristram, who had never bought
property of his own, or so much as contemplated doing so.
One of the Gulf-front homes, in Sarasota, was listed at
$2,400,000; another at $3,900,000!) There were scribbled
calculations in the margins, in pencil, and names and
initials—*Eloise, Martha, Mary Kaye, S.W., Sondra.* The racetrack sheets were even more annotated, and certain races
marked with stars, asterisks, and exclamation points. Tristram, who knew very little about professional racing, still less

about gambling, was mystified by such names as Dazzle, Bullet, Mitzie, Zinger, Dark Star, Boro-Boro, Mutiny Lobell, Maelynne Lobell, Lamb Chop, and Gouge. It took him a while to figure out that some were the names of horses (both thoroughbred and standardbred) and some were the names of greyhound dogs.

By the look of the minute calculations on the sheets it seemed conclusive that Angus T. Markham was a professional gambler; or, at any rate, a dedicated one. What connection was there between the racetrack calculations, the real estate calculations, the women's perfumed letters . . . ? Tristram felt a small thrill of moral rectitude and disapproval; he knew gambling to be a dangerous pastime, a predilection that could shade into an addiction, and then, like alcoholism, into a ravaging disease. It does not matter so much whether one wins but only that, by any possible means, however desperate, one continues to play the game.

Tristram went to the closet and examined the bowler hat and the cane. The hat was from a London haberdashery, and fitted his head rather loosely. (He had not been able to resist a childlike impulse to try it on.) The cane, a sleek gleaming ebony, was heavier than it looked, with a carved-ivory lion's head for a handle. The man is a dandy, Tristram thought, amused. He pulled one of Markham's coats off its hanger and slipped it on, smiling at himself in the mirror. The coat was dark blue linen with wide lapels and brass buttons, finely cut, custom-made and very expensive. Tristram wondered if lapels of so dramatic a width were in style? And brass buttons? His own sports coats and suits, years old, were, he supposed, much the worse for wear, and he had no idea to what style they aspired, if any. Buying clothing, even so much as thinking about buying clothing, rarely preoccupied him. In fact, the last item of clothing he had purchased was his dark gray pinstriped suit, the very suit he had worn to his mother's funeral. . . . As if quarreling with the absent Markham, he said aloud, reprovingly, "This sort of thing is so superficial after all. It does not touch the soul."

Still, it was the first time in a very long time that Tristram had regarded his mirrored reflection with interest; and some admiration; with, in fact, anything other than embarrassed timidity. In a sudden boyish animation he strode about the room, bowler hat atop his head at a jaunty angle, shining black cane crooked through his arm, eyes fixed on the man in the mirror. His heart beat quickly, as if he were onstage. It was all absurd, preposterous, and yet. . . . He *did* look striking, handsome; a man in the exuberant prime of life; in full control of his destiny.

Tristram brought the rim of the bowler hat forward, over his forehead. To the victor go the spoils.

Still, he must make it a point to speak with the manager when he went down for dinner, and ask him to send a bell-boy to the room, to take away Markham's belongings. The confusion of identities must not go any further.

And there was another party whom he'd meant to speak with, over the telephone, that day. . . . But he could not remember. The name had temporarily slipped his mind.

Tristram bathed; and shaved; dressed, in no hurry; sipping from a glass of chilled sherry as he did so, and nibbling Brazil and cashew nuts. Several times he interrupted his toilet to examine the glass eye again, which he had placed atop the bureau, for safekeeping, in a marble ashtray; and to consider another time the contents of Markham's valise, which he had laid out in tidy, discrete piles on the bureau. There was no connection between the glass eye (with its look of willful, even perverse sightlessness) and Markham's things, yet, by their very juxtaposition, in both space and time, one might almost . . . one might almost, if one were so inclined, assume a connection.

Yet, in practical terms, was there any significant connection between the items in Markham's valise? The real estate material with its marginal calculations . . . the racetrack material with its more elaborate calculations . . . the women's love letters (for surely they were love letters) so tactlessly held together by ordinary rubber bands. And *The Rubaiyat* with its much-thumbed and smudged pages. . . . What did these things mean? Did they in fact have "meaning" at all? In the singular, or in the plural? And was the meaning significant? And even if the meaning were significant to the unknown Markham, would it be so to Tristram Heade? Would it prove worth the effort, if he puzzled it out?—instructive, edifying, enlightening?—life-enhancing?

Tristram examined the glass eye again; leafed idly through the real estate brochures. The sad dead stale perfume of the women's letters pinched his nostrils. What a puzzle it was! And what emotions it aroused, both of excitement, and fatigue! Though among Tristram's collection in Richmond were a number of classic mysteries, including rare first editions of *The Hound of the Baskervilles, The Moonstone*, and *The Lair of the White Worm*, he had never much cared for the genre; he had read very few mysteries in his lifetime, and these with virtually none of the respect he held for "serious" literature. The genre struck him as gamesmanship, merely; built upon trickery, often of the flimsiest sort; unpalatable in its violence, which was likely to occur at a moment's notice, with hardly more than a moment's consequence in moral and emotional terms. The form descended from Poe in particular offended him, since it seemed to whip up complications, and horrors, with no end other than that of entertainment: *effect* was all, *significance* null. Each time Tristram read a mystery novel he did, it's true, continue to the very last sentence, but then he invariably slammed the book shut with a sense of being cheated. Real life is simply not like this, he thought. Real life is dense, muddled, in defiance of chronology, and fraught with consequence.

Yet he had to confess that, since the intrusion of "mystery" into his own life (however minor it was, and surely soon to be solved), he had begun to feel his pulses quicken at the mere prospect of the future; not with apprehension, though there was that, to a degree, but rather with simple interest. What will happen next?—assuming, of course, that something will, or must, happen next. He understood that his life, being "real," thus not contained, or concocted, within the bookish genre of mystery, might not involve a satisfactory solution of his situation; yet, at the same time, however irrationally, he could not accept that it might not, if for no other reason than his unexamined assumption of the conventions of the mystery-genre—*however discredited in his own eyes.*

He knew, for instance, that it was unthinkable there might be a connection between his chance finding of the glass eye on Delancy Street (Tristram had made a note of location) and the Markham/Heade confusion of identities. And yet . . .

No. It *was* absurd.

He was standing at a window overlooking Rittenhouse Square, and, beyond it, a dreamlike grid of city streets, each defined by a concatenation of lights. Here is the essence of *city*, Tristram thought, with a strange sense of exhilaration. It does not matter which city, only that there is a city, and impersonality, and adventure, and "newness." On other visits to Philadelphia, Tristram quickly became homesick; or, in any case, he missed the comfort of his long-established bachelor's routine, and was eager to return. This time, however, he felt not the slightest tinge of homesickness. It seemed to him that he had been gone for at least a week . . . but he was in no hurry to return.

Dressing, Tristram found himself absentmindedly knotting a necktie he did not recognize. It was a parrot-bright paisley; it must have been one of Markham's . . . mixed together, by the chambermaid, with his own. After a moment's hesitation, he decided to wear it anyway. Perhaps "A. T. M." would not mind. Perhaps "A. T. M." would never know.

Though from a certain perspective Tristram had wasted the entire day, and remembered, too late, whom he'd meant to telephone,—poor bedridden Uncle Morris Heade: how *could* he have forgotten!—his sense of physical well-being only deepened as he ate his dinner. If anything, the maitre d', the head waiter, and the wine steward were more attentive to him than they had been the previous night; the lavish dinner, with an added course (an extra appetizer, Tristram being unable to decide between oysters Rockefeller and Polynesian tiger shrimp) was even more impressive. And the wines . . . ah, the wines! . . . Tristram made a note to see if they were available, back home.

Out of habit he had brought a book along to dinner, which he remembered to open only at the very last, while sipping at a glass of deliciously potent Austrian liqueur. . . .

There was the Door to which I found no Key:
There was the Veil through which I could not see:
    Some little talk awhile of Me and Thee
There was—and then no more talk of Thee and Me.

That night, drifting off to sleep, Tristram saw dreamlike flashes of the Heade home in Richmond; those quarters he had retained as his own; his bachelor's bedroom in particular, attractive enough, though rather crowded with furnishings, bookshelves, books. He felt a tinge of homesickness after all. Or was it another, yet more powerful emotion . . . a sense of loss, deprivation? He lay in the king-sized canopied bed in the Louis Quatorze suite of the Hotel Moreau, Rittenhouse Square, Philadelphia, while at the same time he lay in his smaller, uncanopied bed at Royalston Place, Richmond, his slightly accelerated pulse beating, beating, as if there might be no end to it, or him. *Myself am Heav'n and Hell.*

Yet there came, as if from a distance, a knocking at the door. (In Richmond? In Philadelphia?) Tristram did not want to hear it, did not want to answer it, did *not* want to wake out of his exhausted, delicious sleep; but finally had no choice. He was sitting up in bed, blinking and staring into the darkness, his heart beating painfully hard in his chest. Was he in Richmond, or was he in Philadelphia? For a moment, he really could not remember.

He switched on the bedside lamp. It was 1:15 A.M.; he

had gone to bed shortly before midnight. The knocking continued, not so loud as it had sounded in his sleep, not nearly so percussive, but rather tentative, muffled. It came not from the door to this room but from the door in the other room, leading into the suite's parlor. "Who is it?" Tristram called out. "Yes? Who is there?"

There was the briefest of pauses, and then the knocking began again, this time more urgently. It will be a woman, Tristram thought. One of his women. He saw that there was nothing to be done but answer the door.

II

1 By the age of thirty-five Tristram Heade had become what is known rather condescendingly as a "confirmed bachelor." (Which did not rule him out from being, in the eyes of certain parties, an "eligible bachelor" as well.) In his imagination he still saw himself in the conventional, yet romantic role of American husband, father, homeowner, citizen; like a man who believes himself an intrepid explorer of the brotherhood of Magellan, Marco Polo, and Admiral Perry, yet whose explorations are confined to the tracing of imaginary voyages on maps drawn up by others, Tristram naively yet hopefully spoke of "someday marrying" or, no less vaguely, of "finding the right woman." Or, with a frowning little smile: "I suppose I really mean a woman who would have *me.*"

Of course he hoped for children too. Particularly sons, to carry on the family name. But the purely physical (that is, the purely sexual) channel by which children must come into the world was daunting to him, to consider. For Tristram had had very few sexual experiences in his life, and none had been altogether satisfying.

Yet women liked him; were drawn to him; confided in him, asked advice of him, sought sympathy from him. The mothers of Richmond debutantes whose seasons were rapidly receding particularly sought him out, in those years when Tristram accepted invitations more readily. It was noted that, living alone in his parents' house, Tristram was becoming, by degrees, rather unsociable and reclusive. But he remained a Virginia Heade, after all, and therefore a person of importance: the last living male issue of a stock descended from Erasmus Heade, the Revolutionary War general; a gentleman to his fingertips; courteous, soft-spoken, modest, and irreproachable in his morals. Not a handsome man in the usual sense of the word he was nonetheless attractive in his big-boned, rather self-conscious way; he was the kind of man at whom people stare, bemused, or frankly perplexed, as if trying to remember his name. He had the look of being someone's cousin: a *presence* mysteriously lacking *identity*.

"It is as if my normal life, my 'real' life, had somehow been deflected from me," Tristram once said, in a fumbling attempt to explain himself to a young female cousin named Abigail, who had taken a kindly interest in him. " 'Deflected'—how? By who?" Abigail asked. "That's just it,—I don't know how, and I don't know by who," Tristram said, shrugging. Abigail looked at him quizzically, as if he were a riddle to be deciphered. She was a very pretty girl, engaged to a West Point cadet, and primed for all that life, in the social class to which she belonged both by birth and temperament, had to offer. "But what exactly do you mean, Tristram?" Abigail asked. "You have a 'real' life somewhere else, and your life now, your life here, as the Tristram we all know, is false? Or your life here is the only life you know, and the other is—what? Lost? Inaccessible?" Tristram smiled in embarrassment, eager to change the subject. "I don't know," he said simply. "It all happened before I was born."

Though his family's fortune had dwindled over the years, with a rude, precipitous drop in the late 1970s, it seemed to be known about town that Tristram had inherited enough to live comfortably on, if he had wished to live comfortably; he could marry if he chose, and support a wife and children, even without working as a lawyer. He had stopped attending services since his mother's death, but remained a financially supportive member of the First Episcopal Church of Richmond; this held him in good stead with the community. He was known to have no vices, no bad habits, no eccentricities . . . at least, no eccentricities not amenable to reform.

"If Tristram would only marry," his mother said, in her final, exhausting illness, when she spoke tactlessly, sometimes even recklessly, sensing how little time remained, "—all might yet be well. But he must *hurry*. After I am gone he will need someone to *take over*."

Tristram's mother had loved him very much; and Tristram had loved his mother. Yet, in the months following her death, he began to forget her; as, to his surprise, and dismay, he'd forgotten his father shortly after *his* death. I mean to be a dutiful son, Tristram thought,—but what is my duty?

It was strange, how, in the two or three rooms of the twenty-room house (a small mansion, really) at Royalston Place, which constituted Tristram's house-within-a-house, he seemed to thrive, like a tough, sinewy, weedy plant. Chicory, perhaps: the hardiest of weeds, growing in thin dirt, or in gravel, yet with sky-blue flowers of exquisite beauty. While others may have worried over him, Tristram never worried about himself because he did not think overmuch about *himself.* A cloistered life has the advantage of silence, and silence spares us echoes. The primary focus of a day spent at Royalston Place was nearly always the arrival of the morning's mail, which, delivered anywhere between ten-thirty and noon, rarely failed to contain a bookdealer's catalogue or brochure, or a letter from a fellow collector. (Tristram wrote regularly to some twenty-odd people, all men, only a few of whom he had actually met.) Of course, the most exciting days were those when Tristram received a new purchase, ordered and paid for by mail. The 1722 edition of *Tyburn Calendar; or Malefactor's Bloody Register,* published by Swindell's of Hanging Bridge, London; a 1685 edition of Dryden's *Tyrannic Love*; a 1778 edition of the anonymous English translation of *The Infamous History of "Count*

Cagliostro"—at such times Tristram's happiness was direct and unbounded as a child's.

His parents did indeed rapidly recede into the past, like comets hurtling themselves into an unfathomable ether. In time they became confused in Tristram's book-bemused memory with his grandparents; and they, with *their* parents, whom Tristram had not known, of course, except as daguerreotypes and family legend had preserved them. Similarly, both sides of the family, his mother's (her maiden name was Buchanan: she too was descended from an illustrious ancestor, a confidant of George Washington's during his presidency) and his father's, became confused in his memory; as things, valuable in themselves, like cuff links, gold watches, tie clips, and the like, seem to lose their value by being jumbled together in a drawer. (Like certain drawers in Tristram's quarters, in fact.)

Tristram's interest in antiquarian books began in early adolescence, when, overweight and shy to the point of pain, he spent a good deal of time in his grandfather Heade's library; a walnut-paneled book-lined place of enormous solace and comfort. Books, Tristram quickly learned, were his friends: they never failed in time of need. Miserable at the prospect of, or, what was worse, the fresh memory of, his clumsiness at one or another tea-dance or family gathering, he could hide himself in his grandfather's library for hours at a time. His father did not approve, of course; it was Mr. Heade's directive that guided Tristram to the University of Virginia, for his undergraduate work, and law school. But books, as they are our friends, are not jealous lovers, who forsake us for having forsaken them: while Tristram tried his hand (or his brain) at the wise, adept, fairly cruel ways of the world, he knew in his innermost heart that his truer life was elsewhere, awaiting him.

And so indeed it was. Or seemed to be, until the arrival of Fleur Grunwald in his life.

Tristram Heade had had his share, since adolescence, of those elusive yet candidly erotic "masculine" dreams whose

point of waking is orgasm; though they had reached a frenzied peak in his late teens he was plagued by them still, at
a time in his life when he believed himself too mature (and
too intelligent) for such fantasies. Waking, in his bed, after
one of these dreams, he would lie very still, in a paralysis of
shame; and distress; in the aftermath of a purely physical
sensation too powerful to be called, simply, "pleasure." Indeed, Tristram found very little pleasure in it.

But if I marry, I should say *when* I marry, it will be different, he thought. For then of course there would be a real
woman in his arms, and not a phantasm that vanished upon
waking.

And he would love this woman in a normal, daylight fashion, as husbands love their wives.

Doomed to sleeplessness at such times, Tristram would
leave his bed, and wander barefoot about the house . . .
passing out of the quarters he retained as his into the
"other" part of the house . . . which, since his mother's
death, he had begun quite consciously to think of as
"other." As if the very house he had inherited was a stranger's, trespassed at risk. Yet, the memory of an erotic embrace, a sexual union, explosive if unwished, and violently
powerful, if distasteful, drove him forward. He was too excited, still, to sleep! He would never sleep again!

Of course the house was empty. But: might she be waiting for him somewhere upstairs?—in one of the closed-off
rooms?

Whoever "she" was.

But of course "she" did not exist.

Or, granted her possible existence, "she" did not exist
in terms of Tristram Joseph Heade.

Though he suffered from a mild night blindness, and
had difficulty seeing clearly on these nocturnal prowls, Tristram carried a candle to light his way; a flashlight would
have seemed too practical . . . too unromantic. He smiled a
sick, crooked, abashed smile, grateful to be alone, thus un-
perceived, by those who would have pitied him or feared
for his sanity. He knew of course that there was no one in

the house, in any of the rooms, not his parents' bedroom, not his mother's sewing room, not the upstairs sitting room, not the numerous guest rooms . . . yet, stubbornly, he continued on his rounds, his candle held defiantly aloft and his heart kicking against his ribs. His senses were alert to the smallest, most muffled sounds: the scurrying of tiny clawed feet overhead (mice?); a low hoarse whispering (the wind under the eaves?); a sound as of folds of silk rubbed harshly together (curtains? somehow stirred by the wind?). One night he entered a room unused for years, in which, as family legend would have it, a visiting cousin (female) scandalously entertained a young man (in some versions a Confederate Army lieutenant, in other versions merely "a young man"), and heard, or believed he heard, an exchange of whispers, and a startled little spasm of giggles . . . and smelled an odor of violets, old, stale, yet somehow poignant . . . though of course the room was empty: nothing except a few items of furniture, covered in lugubrious white shrouds. Upon another, more disturbing occasion Tristram entered the old billiards room, Mr. Heade's hideaway as Mrs. Heade had tolerantly called it, and saw, to his astonishment, a single playing card, the queen of spades, lying on the carpetless floor. . . . Tristram picked the card up, puzzled, noting that, though not new, it was still shiny; and not covered with the acrid layer of dust that covered the floor itself. His sensitive nostrils also detected a faint smell of pipe tobacco; and, out of place in this most masculine of settings, a woman's perfume . . . rich, heady, over-sweet . . . a strident scent very different from the genteel, girlish scent of violets.

Tristram wondered: had his father had a secret woman friend?—a "mistress"?—one of the servant-girls, perhaps? The thought was immensely disturbing; it both repelled and excited him. Though he could scarcely remember the man who had been his father, he did, suddenly, recall the pungent odor of his pipe tobacco; and his own hope, as a boy, that he too would smoke a pipe someday; his father's very pipe, and his father's very brand of tobacco: "Old Bugler."

Suddenly frightened, Tristram backed hurriedly out of the room. His hands shook and his eyes filled with moisture. In the hallway, in flight, he imagined he heard a throaty sort of laughter behind him . . . but it must have been, of course, the wind. The wind in the eaves.

2 Tristram was hurriedly knotting the cord of the quilted-silk black robe when he noticed that the robe was no item of apparel he knew. It was a beautiful Japanese-style kimono, not at all like his ordinary flannel robe; it must have belonged to Markham. He had pulled it from a hanger in the closet without looking.

"Just a minute, please! I'm coming."

The knocking at the door continued with increased urgency, as if Tristram's call hadn't been heard; and when he opened the door he saw on the threshold the most extraordinary young woman. . . . No one Tristram knew, and no one who knew him; yet her face, her eyes, the very set of her mouth seemed familiar to him. She was breathless as if she had come a long distance to his door, at enormous risk.

He seemed to know, too, what she would say, before she spoke.

"Angus . . . ? It *is* Angus?"

Tristram made an effort to smile, though stricken to the heart. "I'm afraid you have the wrong room. The wrong man."

"But—isn't it Angus? Angus Markham?"

The breathless young woman wore a wide-rimmed hat of some smart, black-glazed material; a thin black veil obscured yet did not quite hide her enormous eyes, which appeared to be brimming with moisture, or with intense feeling: fixed upon Tristram, as if willing him to be that other, absent man, their gaze was almost more than he could bear. "But Angus it *is* you . . . isn't it?" she pleaded. "If you're angry with me . . . I know, I know you have every right to be angry with me. . . . Please don't be: oh please! I have no one but you.''

"But I—"

"I know I disappointed you in Saratoga Springs. Like a high-bred filly, you said, who bolts her first important race. And now . . . as you see . . . I am paying for it. Please don't turn me away! I am terrified someone has seen me come here.''

So Tristram invited her inside, and shut the door quickly after her; all the while trying to explain that, though he and Angus Markham resembled each other to an uncanny degree, they were two quite different and distinct individuals.

But the young woman seemed not to hear. She continued to stare at him with an expression of such childlike yearning and hope, and guileless adoration, he felt his senses reel. How lucky, the absent Markham! With trembling fingers she lifted the translucent veil from her eyes, which were brimming with tears; brightly dark eyes with long curving lashes; set wide and deep in her rather moon-shaped face, the whites perfectly white and the irises a hazy golden brown, like miniature suns. Her mouth was small, the upper lip particularly short, but beautifully shaped; her nose long, slender, narrow at the tip. Tristram was reminded of a doll's face—one of those painted porcelain dolls of the previous century, whose fussy, lace-trimmed velvet and silk costumes were sewed by hand, by genteel ladies with a good deal of leisure and a love of small, pretty, charming things.

It is she, he thought. A queer smile tugged at his lips; the sick, crooked smile of his nocturnal quests.

"You *do* remember, don't you, Angus?" she said. "Fleur Grunwald . . . to whom you were once so kind? For whom you once . . . seemed to feel some affection?"

Tristram drew his breath in slowly; made every effort to speak calmly, reasonably. He said, "I'm sure that Markham would remember you, Mrs. Grunwald, but, as I've tried to explain, I am not the man; *I am not Angus Markham.*"

" 'Mrs. Grunwald'! Angus, how can you!"

She flinched as if Tristram had struck her; indicating, with girlish hurt and reproach, the left-hand lapel of Tristram's resplendent black robe—on which the initials *A. T. M.* were prominently embossed. Tristram felt the blood rush hotly into his face as if he had been caught in a lie.

"The initials on the robe are misleading," Tristram said. "I . . . there is an explanation . . . but I am *not* . . . the man you seek."

He was standing foursquare before the door, however, blocking the young woman's passage; and made no move to step aside. He thought again, It *is* she.

Confused, blinking dazedly, as if she understood nothing Tristram had said, or was incapable of grasping its significance in relationship to her entreaty, she said, "I had known you could be playful, Angus, but I hadn't known you could be cruel. Or would want to be, with me."

Tristram said quickly, "*I* am not playful, I assure you, Mrs. Grunwald! *I* am not cruel."

"But why do you call me by *his* name?" she asked naively. Her eyes, widened, round, were fixed upon Tristram's with a look of stupefaction, as if she were in a state of exhaustion, or hypnotized. "Aren't I Fleur to you any longer?"

There lifted from her clothing and hair a faint, wild fragrance of lily-of-the-valley, that pierced Tristram's senses with its sweetness; and drew moisture to his eyes. She repeated, *"Aren't I Fleur to you any longer?"* and when Tristram did not answer said, "You were right, Angus. 'You will be desperate to leave him some day,' you said, 'when perhaps it will be too late.' "

Tristram said helplessly, "But why . . . are you desperate? Is it . . . ?"

"Angus, are you mocking me?"

"Of course I'm not mocking you."

"Yet you seem to want me to humble myself before you," she said, shaking her head in disbelief. "As if you are not

YOU CAN'T CATCH ME 47

the man of honor, the gentleman, you are. As if, in a night-mare, you are someone else.''

Tristram wanted very badly suddenly to take the young woman's hands in his; to give what comfort he could. Yet he could not accept it, that, on the basis of a misunderstand-ing, he had any right to touch her: if it was Angus Markham she wanted, and not Tristram Heade? No, there was no choice, no honorable alternative: ''Mrs. Grunwald, I must insist that I am *not* Angus Markham; I am not your friend. That is, I am not . . . Angus Markham. Nor do I know Mark-ham. Nor do I know where he is.''

Even now Fleur Grunwald touched a handkerchief to her eyes, and looked searchingly at Tristram, for a dazzlingly long moment. Her lovely eyes! Her flawless skin, which the faintest blemish would have disfigured! And the burnished-brown sheen of her hair, caught up in a twist at the back of her head, from which a few wavy strands escaped, as if caressing her lovely throat. . . . She wore a high-buttoned black dress of some fine light woolen material, with a match-ing jacket whose long puffed sleeves covered not only her wrists but the upper parts of her hands; her many-layered skirt fell nearly to her ankles; her shoes were black patent leather pumps. With her tiny pearl-cluster earrings, and an antique pearl-and-diamond brooch at her throat, and the veiled hat, Fleur Grunwald reminded Tristram of no one so much as one of the well-to-do young matrons of Richmond society, of that world he had seemingly lost.

''Is it 'Mrs. Grunwald'? And you say you are not mocking me?''

Tristram stood mute, and miserable. He and Fleur Grun-wald regarded each other in mutual doubt in a long pained moment charged with imbalance and peril, very like those near-forgotten episodes of Tristram's early adolescence when, stiff and overwarm in formal attire that never seemed to fit correctly, he had had to approach girls with whom he might dance. There was a formula question he had to ask but it had slipped his mind. . . .

Fleur Grunwald was saying, not accusingly so much as in a resigned, matter-of-fact voice, "If this is to punish me, Angus, for having . . . disappointed you, in Saratoga, please know that I have been punished many times over for having refused you when you offered to save me. You were so dear to me, so kind! So generous! To have seen in my face how unhappy I was, in secret,—when no one else, none of his circle, would ever have seen; or seeing, would have offered to help. For Grunwald is a man whom other men admire, and fear, even if they do not like him. And the first Mrs. Grunwald, and the second Mrs. Grunwald, and now the third Mrs. Grunwald . . . are interchangeable to such men. Perhaps," she said, "we *are* interchangeable. And so we are lost."

Tristram said, "No."

"Yet you seem to have forgotten me."

"You must understand . . . that circumstances in my life have changed too," Tristram said.

He spoke blindly; gropingly; scarcely knowing what he said. It was as if someone were urging him forward, not unkindly, though perhaps a bit impatiently, a stranger's hand pressed between his shoulder blades, and pushing. "I . . . am not exactly the man you knew in Saratoga Springs."

"You are married?"

"No. But—"

"You are in love?"

"No."

"You no longer feel, as you once did, about me? —Not that I blame you in the slightest." She paused; and said bitterly, "You are hardly to blame, after all, for my husband's vicious appetites."

Tentatively, blushing, he said, "It *has* been some years . . ."

"But only three! And I thought of you constantly, and treasured your letters! If I never wrote to you, Angus, it was only because . . ." She paused; pressed her handkerchief to her eyes another time; seemed, for a moment, too stricken to continue. ". . . because of certain facts of my marital life . . . of which I cannot speak. Of which, three years ago, I did not feel I could speak out of shame . . . and disgust. And the terror that you, hearing such things, would feel shame and disgust as well . . . and revulsion toward me."

"Revulsion?"

Her head bowed, Fleur Grunwald nodded mutely.

"Revulsion? I? For *you*?"

With no consciousness of what he did, only that, at this time, and in this precise way, it *must* be done, Tristram took gentle hold of the young woman's shoulders (such delicately boned shoulders!), and helped her to be seated on the nearest sofa. With the abandon of a small child Fleur Grunwald began at last to cry, her face hidden in her hands. Yet she held herself stiffly, shyly, with a maidenly sort of apprehension; she gave herself up to her grief, and a terrible grief it was, but did not surrender to Tristram's embrace, as if resisting that very inclination. She has not been, after all, *his* mistress, Tristram thought, with enormous relief.

She wept, and her warm tears splashed on Tristram's hands, and a violent flamelike sensation passed through his body, leaving him weak. He said with sudden passion, "Please don't cry: I give you my word that you will be safe from your husband, and that you will be free of him. *I will protect you with my very life.*"

Only the foyer of the suite was lighted; Tristram was sitting with the sobbing young woman in a shadowy sort of alcove, behind which, magisterially, a tall narrow window opened out onto the ambiguity of a city night—an immense, clear, starlit sky that blended indistinguishably with the lights of the city, and gave to the darkened room a humming sort of radiance. Though Markham might have been more forceful with Fleur Grunwald, and would surely, Tristram suspected, have closed her in his arms (for the distraught young woman *did* want comfort, didn't she? *had* spoken of love, hadn't she?), Tristram contented himself with clasping her gloved hands; leaning close to her, but not overly close; murmuring, as she spoke, words of sympathy and encouragement. How extraordinary this was! How far Tristram Heade had come from his bachelor's life back in Richmond, within a very few days . . . ! For all its acceleration his heart beat happily; his pulses sang. For all that Fleur Grunwald's story turned out to be, even in its fragmentized form, deeply upsetting and repugnant, Tristram could not in his innermost heart regret it, since it had brought her to him; and him to her.

It emerged, over a period of an hour and a half, in halting, piecemeal fashion, that Fleur Grunwald, twenty-three years old, and married since the age of seventeen to a Philadelphia businessman and philanthropist named Otto Grunwald, had finally, after years of abuse, fled his home; dared incur his wrath by making the break he had warned her against making, numberless times, under pain of death. As if, she said, trembling, death were not preferable to her, to continuing to live with *him.*

"Don't ask why I left him now, after so long,—it is too shameful, and too disgusting," Fleur said. "But finally, last Friday, out of desperation that he would do to me what he has, from time to time, hinted of doing, I finally summoned up the courage, and fled; as you had urged me three years ago. I am staying temporarily with a relative of his, a spinster cousin of Grunwald's who has always been sympathetic with me, and will not betray me. But I must leave within a few days, I can't endanger *her* too. Grunwald has spies, he has men in his employ," Fleur said, beginning again to sob, "—there is no escaping him for long, while I am in Philadelphia."

It turned out, to Tristram's surprise, that Fleur was staying in a brownstone on Delancy Street!—by the most remarkable coincidence, the very street on which he had found the glass eye. But of course there could be no connection.

Fleur spoke, agitatedly, and not always coherently; drawing close to, and then shrinking from, an explanation of why she had decided, so abruptly, with so little preparation, to leave Grunwald at this time— "It is too loathsome, it cannot be believed." Tristram feared her fainting; or becoming hysterical; he feared a sudden knock at the door— the vindictive husband, or, what would in fact be more distressing, Angus Markham himself. (For if Markham had contacted the lost and found office of the railway terminal, and the clerk had told him Tristram's name and telephone number, it was not at all improbable the man might show up.) The decision to help Fleur Grunwald, to lay down his life for her, as Tristram had extravagantly sworn, seemed to have brought with it, unexamined, unconsidered,—for in the exigency of the moment, correctly perceived as the turning point in Tristram Heade's life, there was no time for cogitation, or caution!—and no gentleman could have behaved otherwise!—the ancillary decision to assume, for a while, at least, the identity of "Angus Markham": for Tristram understood, were he to insist upon unmasking himself, or, rather, undeceiving Fleur, the humiliated young woman would have fled him immediately.

The deception is only temporary, he thought. And as it is for *her* good, it must be done.

By Fleur's account her husband was a man in his mid- or late fifties, and quite wealthy; not one of Philadelphia's most prodigiously wealthy men; but very well-to-do; like Tristram Heade, the undeserving heir of wealth. Unlike Tristram, however, Grunwald was actively involved in his various investments, and by way of carefully chosen philanthropic projects ("in themselves investments," Fleur said, "for Grunwald does nothing that does not enhance Grunwald") he had enhanced the already honorable name of Grunwald in Philadelphia public life. Grunwald's father and grandfather had both been disagreeable men, Fleur had been given to believe, from tales and anecdotes casually told of them, involved, over the years, in petty family strife and disputes, and a plague of lawsuits. "But from what I sense their moral nature fell within the range of what might be called 'normal,' " Fleur said. "Grunwald's does not."

"I see," Tristram said.

And, "I know."

As, several times, Fleur approached the actual circumstances of her relations with Grunwald, her manner became increasingly agitated and distracted; she spoke vaguely of "systematic abuse," and "tyranny," and "torture," but Tristram did not know whether she spoke literally, or metaphorically; whether Grunwald's cruelty was physical in some way, or simply (though it was wrong to say "simply") psychological. In any case, as clearly as he could determine, it had increased, in recent months, in severity; being related in some mysterious way with Grunwald's health and his fears of growing old; his "terror," as Fleur called it, of the time when his "manly powers" would wane . . . and he, Otto Grunwald, would be reduced to as piteous a figure as Fleur herself.

"My husband is a man who very much pities women, even as he scorns us," Fleur said carefully. "And he is very much attracted to us, even as he is revolted."

Hearing this, Tristram could not suppress a shudder. He wondered what, in the most literal sense, this young woman's words meant.

It was now nearly three o'clock in the morning. Fleur's eyelids drooped with fatigue; her face had become dead-white, as if drained of blood. But when Tristram made the eminently practical suggestion that she try to sleep on the sofa,—he would leave her entirely alone of course, for as long as she wished—she laughed nervously, and protested that she must leave soon; she'd had no intention of staying so long. Even if, as she said, nothing had been decided.

Tristram heard this clearly, but did not know what to make of it.

Had a decision been in the offing?

She stood, and smoothed her hair, and affixed her hat (which had slipped from her head); adjusted, with an air of embarrassment and impatience, her slightly rumpled clothing; insisting that she must leave, and would see him the following day. "When we know more clearly what course we can take," she said. "When . . . when we know more clearly."

Again, Tristram did not understand. He sensed that Fleur Grunwald's meaning was something very clear, in fact, in itself, eminently practical; yet it eluded him, as, reaching with naive directness for something glimpsed behind us, in a mirror, we feel our fingers closing in empty air.

Fleur prepared to leave, and Tristram said, puzzled, "At least let me accompany you back to Delancy Street, won't you? It will take only a minute for me to put on some street clothes. Will you wait? You can't possibly leave here alone, Fleur, even to take a taxi, in the condition you're in."

"I came here alone, after all," Fleur said in a small dull spiritless voice. "I should be capable of leaving alone."

"*Please* wait."

Fleur did not say no; seemed to have said yes. Tristram excused himself, and hurried into the other room, quickly changing his clothes. Where were his shoes? *His* shoes? . . . He was thinking that, had he been Markham, he might be rather hurt by the young woman's abrupt change of mood; might well have been vexed. Of course he did not know Angus Markham but suspected that, unlike Tristram Heade, he was accustomed to sexual conquest; accustomed, in any case, to women who came to him in desperation, knowing that he would know to help. And how?

When he returned to the parlor, however, having been away no more than three or four minutes at the most, it was to discover that his visitor was gone; leaving no trace of herself behind except a faint scent of lily-of-the-valley, and a neatly printed little note affixed with a hat pin to the back of the sofa:

---

997 Delancy
DO NOT COME TILL AFTER NIGHTTIME

---

3 By nighttime of the next day, when Tristram Heade presented himself at the front door of the Delancy Street brownstone, and rang the doorbell, he was in a state of nerves of a kind altogether new to him: yet oddly calm: outwardly calm: thinking, This is Markham's way, and it must be mine as well.

He had spent much of the day making inquiries into Mr. Otto Grunwald; had hired a taxi to take him into the wealthy neighborhood, contiguous with Fairmount Park, in which Grunwald lived; had walked numerous times past the property pointed out to him as Grunwald's—several acres of meticulously tended lawns and gardens, at the rear of which, beyond a wrought-iron fence with a medieval-looking gate, a French Normandy mansion seemed to rise with the eerie plausibility of a dream within a dream. The Heades of Virginia had been conspicuously wealthy, in their time; but here, Tristram thought, chastened, here is real wealth.

He felt some rage too: an infusion of Angus Markham's spirit perhaps. Or was it his own? He had fallen in love with the beautiful young wife of the man who lived in that house; the beautiful young wife who had been held a virtual captive for years, in that house. And what could he do? What *would* he do?

It is too loathsome, it cannot be believed.

From all that Tristram had been able to learn, by way of questions put to various persons—among them the manager of the Hotel Moreau, and several antiquarian bookdealers whose shops he visited that day, and a Buchanan

cousin who was a partner in one of the city's most presti-
gious law firms—it seemed that Otto Grunwald, no matter
the mysterious secret depravity of his soul, did have a reputation in Philadelphia as one of the more faithful and generous members of the "private sector." Among his charities
were the Philadelphia Symphony, the Philadelphia Museum
of the Arts, the American Red Cross, the American Association for the Advancement of Mental Health, and the Episcopal Hospital, for which he was a trustee. Grunwald was a
trustee too for The Folkes School, to which, for generations,
Grunwalds had sent their sons; sonless himself, Grunwald
gave the school money regularly, and had recently donated
a lavish new building, Grunwald Hall, in memory of his father. Fleur's words sounded in Tristram's head, with a despairing vehemence he had not heard the night before—
Grunwald does nothing that does not enhance Grunwald.

The most disturbing information Tristram learned about
Otto Grunwald was that there had indeed been two young
wives preceding Fleur. The first had died at the age of
twenty-six of an allegedly accidental overdose of sleeping
tablets; the second had died at the age of twenty-four of
injuries sustained after a fall down a flight of stairs in her
home.

("But were no charges ever brought against Grunwald?"
Tristram asked his cousin, with whom he spoke on the telephone, and the man said in a flat, bemused voice, "Against
Otto Grunwald? In this city? On little or no evidence? For
a man with a degree from Virginia you seem to know very
little about the law, Tristram.")

After Fleur Grunwald left his hotel room Tristram had been
able to sleep only fitfully. Several times he woke to see the
young woman in the room with him, her face very pale and
her eyes very wide, shining with tears. *Aren't I Fleur to you
any longer?* Her voice was wild, sweet, pleading, edged with
terror.

Tristram, in love for the first time in his life, waited impatiently for the day to pass. He wondered if early dusk

qualified as "nighttime" and decided that it did; it must. Well before that time he set out for Delancy Street, and arrived at the address he wanted while the sun was still in the western sky, a furious fiery orange.

The street was unusually wide for a residential street in this part of the city, and its houses were unusually large, each three storeys high, made of fine old brownstone in excellent condition. Plane trees lined both sides of the street and in the carefully tended strip of lawn in front of 997 there grew a number of elegantly trimmed evergreen shrubs. By the time Tristram climbed the steps and rang the doorbell he was trembling inwardly and felt moisture at the back of his neck. Calm, he told himself. Be calm.

When a silent black servant answered the door, Tristram identified himself as, simply, "Markham: the man Mrs. Grunwald is expecting." He was led immediately up a flight of stairs and into a room in which Fleur awaited him, on her feet, looking toward him with an expression of eagerness and apprehension. Her immediate words were, "Angus! Have you . . . ?" Tristram, puzzled, did not know how to reply. He took one of her small-boned hands, which felt rather cold and moist, and impulsively lifted it to his lips. "My dear Fleur," he whispered. "My poor girl." It was Tristram speaking, or it was Markham, and the words sounded right, or nearly. Fleur shivered; laughed nervously, like a young girl; and drew away, even as, in virtually the same motion, she seemed about to step forward into Tristram's embrace. Tristram thought, She is a woman terrified of men: of a man's touch, even in love.

He thought, Grunwald must pay for this.

Fleur asked him to be seated, and the silent black servant left them alone. The room in which they sat was an old-fashioned drawing room, beautifully paneled in cherry-wood, with a bay window overlooking the street below; a small cheery fire burned in a fireplace. Again Fleur Grunwald wore black, this evening a floor-length robe or negligee of a sumptuous silken material, richly embroidered, with a high mandarin collar, numerous tiny buttons, and long flowing sleeves. Her hair, an ashy shade of brown, naturally wavy, and rather thin, was parted neatly in the center of her head and gathered up smoothly at the nape of her neck with a mother-of-pearl comb. To mitigate her pallor she had daubed powder onto her face, and reddened her lips; she wore no jewelry except, surprisingly, on the third finger of her left hand, an enormous square-cut diamond with a matching wedding band studded with smaller diamonds.

Tristram asked suddenly, "That robe, Fleur, is very beautiful, but is it yours?"—a question that took both Fleur and himself by surprise. Fleur laughed nervously again, and stared at him in perplexity. "—I mean, because it's one or two sizes too large for you," Tristram said, "I thought it might belong to your cousin." Fleur said, blushing, "I feel more comfortable with clothes that are loose-fitting. I don't like *tight* things."

As if to change the subject Fleur offered Tristram a glass of sherry, which he accepted, with gratitude; and poured herself a glass as well, lifting it to her lips with fingers that trembled slightly. Tristram had the idea that this very young woman was not much accustomed to drinking; and that, though she made an effort (as he was making an effort) to appear calm, she was really quite agitated. He said, clearing his throat, "I hope your husband didn't try to contact you today," and Fleur said, after a moment, with a shy, strange smile, "I had thought *you* might have contacted *him* . . . but it seems you did not?" Tristram said slowly, "No. I did not." His face burned as if this were a shameful admission.

Fleur made no reply, her eyes downcast. She held her sherry glass to her mouth with both hands, as a child might; but was not drinking. Tristram said, with sudden conviction, "I will see him tomorrow, Fleur. I know where he lives." Silent, Fleur appeared to be holding herself very still. A grandfather clock ticked coolly in a corner of the room. Tristram said, "I'll insist upon seeing him tomorrow. All this will have to be worked out."

"Yes," Fleur said softly, stifling a sob, "—it will have to be worked out."

Seeing the young woman's eyes fill with tears, and her delicate mouth tremble, Tristram was stricken to the heart. He set his glass down hurriedly and took her hand, both her hands, in his. He whispered passionately, "I love you. I do want to help you. I will do anything for you."

Fleur gave an involuntary little cry of surprise or fright at Tristram's sudden gesture. Her natural instinct was to shrink from him but she forced herself (so Tristram sensed, to his chagrin) to remain still and unresisting. She was trembling badly but she said, in a small hushed voice, "I love you too, Angus. As you know. I . . . I love you too . . . as you know."

"My darling, don't be frightened! I won't hurt you."

"Oh I know, I know," she whispered. She allowed him to kiss her on the cheek, sitting very still, ramrod straight in her chair. "I know, Angus . . . *you* would not."

Though weak with desire Tristram knew he must restrain himself. How like a wild animal she was, a young doe, quavering in his arms! And how brutally Grunwald must have treated her, to have frightened her so! The conviction rang suddenly in Tristram's head—*You must kill the man, you have no choice.*

Fleur struggled to her feet, and backed away, shaking her head, murmuring, "No. No. No," as if Tristram, or another person, had spoken aloud. In a high rapid voice she said, "I think you should leave now, Angus. I think this is a wrong time. I don't feel well. I feel very tired. My head aches. My eyes. My body. I am his wife,—I am a married woman. I am his. I am his by law. I think you should leave now. Please leave. Now. *Please.*" Tristram followed her, scarcely knowing what he did, taking hold of her arm, towering over her as she cringed before him, saying, "Fleur, what do you mean? You asked me to come here, and I've come, and I do want to help, and I *will* help,—you know I adore you—" Fleur tried to push him away, sobbing; Tristram held her fast; hoping, with that part of his brain that seemed to have detached itself from their struggle, that he would not lose control. *She invited you here; she came to your hotel room; she has offered herself; she is yours for the taking.* . . . These words sounded strangely in Tristram's ears.

"Leave me alone! Don't *touch* me,—I cannot bear to be *touched*!"

Tristram released the terrified woman, and stood back from her, to show her he meant no harm. He was panting and his face burned with a complex of emotions: frustration, shame, sexual desire. He felt oversized and clumsy; oafish as a performing bear; in, even, the attractive outfit he had assembled out of his and Markham's clothes . . . Tristram's shirt and well-worn trousers, Markham's blue linen coat and blue-striped tie. He began to apologize, and offered to leave at once, should she want him to leave, when Fleur started to weep uncontrollably, and begged him *not* to leave— "I have no one but you, Angus. *I have no one but you.*" It was a cri de coeur of such despairing passion, Tristram felt the very hairs on the back of his neck stir. Yet when he tried to embrace her, again, to his astonishment, she pushed him away; murmuring "No, no, *no*—" She wrenched herself free of him, fell against a chair, fell to the carpet, shook her head violently from side to side, thrashing about as if overcome by a seizure of some kind. Tristram looked on, horrified. Was the young woman an epileptic? Was she mad? "Fleur, my darling," he said, offering to help her up, and she said, raving, slapping at his hand, "Get away! Don't touch me! No one dares touch me! I cannot bear it!"

Then she fainted; and lay very still.

And lay in that posture—head turned to one side, eyes shut tight, jaws clenched—for the space of some seconds, while Tristram crouched over her, repeating her name. He dared not unbutton the collar of Fleur's robe, dared not loosen the sash knotted at her waist. . . . After a moment she began to revive, however; blinking dazedly, as if waking from a long sleep. She stared up at Tristram, at first without recognition; finally whispered, "Angus—of course it is *you*." She grasped Tristram's arm, lifted herself into his arms, slowly, unsteadily, and allowed him to help her to a chair.

She brushed her hair out of her flushed face, took several deep breaths, and, to Tristram's astonishment, began to rock slowly to and fro, speaking in a low, throaty, singsong, seductive voice, her eyes fixed upon his face. "I am Zoe. I am here to speak the truth. This is the truth *she* will not speak, because she is such a little girl. But I am Zoe and I am here to speak the truth and Zoe tells only the truth because the truth is all that Zoe knows."

With one part of his brain Tristram was utterly astounded; with another, rather more intrigued; not, strangely, so very surprised. He pulled up a chair close beside the disheveled young woman and said, gently, "Yes, Zoe. It *is* Angus. Tell him the truth."

4 There followed then a remarkable hour during which, in a childlike yet sensual singsong voice, very different, in its cadence, modulation, and tone, from Fleur Grunwald's voice, yet at the same time unmistakably hers, "Zoe" confessed to Tristram the bizarre details of her marital life; truths of a sort Tristram could never have imagined, let alone hypothesized in terms of Fleur Grunwald. For it was not to be believed! But it was to be believed!

"You see. *His* work. You see? *His.*"

As Tristram stared, Zoe slowly raised her right arm, as if defiantly; allowing the sleeve to slide down; revealing,—was it a tattoo? Tattoos?

"*His* work," Zoe said.

"What on earth—?"

"No! Don't touch!"

"But, Fleur—"

"No," Zoe said curtly. "Don't touch."

"But Fleur—"

"I am *Zoe.*"

"But what has happened to you?"

Tristram went to her, to examine her other arm; but Zoe shrank from him. "No," she said. "Zoe will speak." She paused, licking her lips. Tristram's response had clearly gratified her. "Zoe *knows* and Zoe will *speak.*"

Her eyes fixed almost greedily on Tristram's face, Zoe raised her right arm; and again her sleeve slid down, revealing, to Tristram's horror, another elaborate, multicolored tattoo. "My God," Tristram whispered, "—are you

tattooed like that over your entire body? Is that your secret?''

"Zoe will tell you what Zoe wants to tell you."

"My poor darling—''

"Since *she* sleeps, Zoe will speak. *She,*—the piteous little
fool.''

Tristram was staring incredulously at the young woman's
arms, which she held out, in the lamplight, with a curious
sort of disdainful pride. She too was, it seemed, fascinated
with her disfigured flesh.

"*His* work,'' she said, smiling.

"You don't mean Grunwald did this? *This?* With a tattooing needle? —It looks almost professional.''

" 'Woman is to be adored,' says He.''

"What a madman!''

"*He* is never mad.''

"Does anyone else know about this? His family—?''

"They know what they know. And what they do not wish
to know they do not know.'' She paused. She laughed, yawning and stretching her arms. "It is a secret of Master's cave.''

"Master's *cave*—?''

Tristram thought it a hellish sight: the intricate, almost
rococo pattern of tattoos in the soft pale flesh of the young
woman's arms: geometrical shapes, grotesquely stylized flowers and vines, hieroglyphic figures of a kind Tristram had
never seen before. (Except perhaps in the margins of medieval or Oriental texts.) Most of the colors were rich and
vibrant, with a look of being heated; red, crimson, yellow,
gold-yellow, emerald-green, turquoise-blue; others appeared
faded. Above the wrists the tattoos ascended in a mad gay
tapestry of interweaving and reticulated forms, an indeci-
pherable code. Tristram could barely speak. "Is there
more?''

Zoe laughed; lay back in the chair, as if on a bed; and,
with a moist mocking smile, began to undo the row of tiny
black buttons. " 'Be still,' says He, 'and you will not be hurt.'
Says He.'' Inside the oversized silk robe Zoe was naked; her
slender, beautiful body grotesquely covered in tattoos.

She laughed again, seeing Tristram's face.

Tristram's first instinct was to hide his eyes; shield his eyes; but of course he could not so much as glance away. Beautiful Fleur Grunwald barbarically disfigured!—it was the most astonishing spectacle he had ever looked upon in his life.

"My God! How can such things be!"

Zoe murmured, as if indifferently, " 'Like God.' Says He."

The symbols stitched into her tender young breasts and belly were sumptuously ornate, exotic; some of them resembling peacock's feathers, with turquoise-blue eyes; jeweled eyes. Tristram blinked: the woman's body was covered in eyes!— They were miniature, nearly hidden in the designs on the arms, then, in the torso, blossoming into life-size: the size of human eyes. He thought of the glass eye on his dresser, and shuddered.

Interlarded with these and other figures were occult symbols, like cuneiform, arranged in verselike patterns of three and four lines. The symbols were almost words; teasingly familiar; like words glimpsed in dreams. Where had he seen such figures before? Had he ever seen them before? Or did he somehow, as in a dream, "remember"?

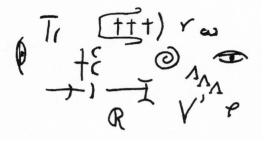

By this time Tristram was kneeling on the carpet before Zoe, spreading open her robe with shaking fingers. He stared; he swallowed hard; it was a feast of a sort, demonically seductive. He said in a choked voice, "What kind of monster is your husband, to have done such a . . . perverse thing?" Zoe said, "He is *her* husband, not mine. Zoe has no one. Zoe is free."

"What do these symbols mean?"

Zoe was allowing Tristram to examine her as if there were not the slightest shyness between them; as if she were not a naked woman, and Tristram not, though clothed, a clearly excited and aroused man. Yet Tristram, always the gentleman, made an effort to control himself; to comport himself with dignity, of a kind; even though the thought ran savagely through his brain, *She is yours now, she has given herself to you, now there can be no going back.*

He considered the hieratic figures stitched so luridly into flesh . . . triangles, octagons, hexagons; dozens of peacock's-tail eyes; these twisting writhing coiling undulating forms. It was a text of a kind but what did it mean?

Each of Zoe's breasts was cupped, from beneath, by a floral design in which words, hieroglyphic and unreadable, were enchased; giving to the soft flesh a marbled, textured appearance that was really quite beautiful. It was hideous, ugly; yet beautiful. That, Tristram thought, swallowing hard, could not be denied. On Zoe's belly, below the navel, were more verselike blocks of symbols, larger and clearer though no more intelligible than elsewhere. He said, "What is the language? What do these words mean?"

"Says He, 'I alone know the charm.' "

Then, in a more sober, accusatory voice, "*She* never dares to look; bathes with her eyes averted, or shut tight; dresses in the dark. Zoe alone dares look, because she is free; but can see herself only by way of a mirror; thus cannot truly see. 'A charm,' says He. 'Writ in a tongue that has long gone by.' "

"And all this . . . mutilation . . . done against your will?"

Zoe laughed as if gaily. "*She* has no will. She is only consent."

"But why didn't you—she—leave him years ago? Why did she ever marry him?"

"She was so young, she knew nothing. She thought, 'Be-

cause I am beautiful, and weak, someone will love me; someone will protect me.' "

Languidly, Zoe stood; stepped away; let the robe fall
slowly from her. She turned, as if coquettishly, to show Tristram her back . . . the slender waist, the hips and buttocks
gently swelling . . . the smooth perfect envelope of flesh
covered in the rococo pattern: figures, flowers, eyes, word-
symbols. Tristram drew in his breath sharply. Zoe said,
taunting, " 'It is love,' says He. Says she, 'O do not hurt
me.' Says she, *begs* she, 'O no' and 'O yes.' "

She went on, in a flatter voice, "Grunwald wants her
beautiful, as he says, in his eyes. For his pleasure. She is a
silly sad little thing who deserves her hurt. . . . So you are
thinking? Yes? So you are thinking?" She paused; Tristram
did not know how to reply. "If it were Zoe and Zoe alone
she would have fled a very long time ago; would have perhaps exacted *her* revenge. Take what you can of the man's
wealth, as other unhappy wives do, fleeing their husbands;
unable to endure the terms of their captivity. If it were Zoe
and Zoe alone she would take such lovers as Angus Markham with no compunction; no hesitation; no conscience.
'Appetite,' says He, 'is all that *is*.' "

Tristram daringly traced with his forefinger a curving
twisting imbricated pattern of flowers, tendrils, vines, and
small staring turquoise-blue eyes that ran the length of Zoe's
back, beginning at her left shoulder and undulating its way
down to her right buttock. He had never seen, he was thinking, a sight more monstrous, yet more beautiful. And this,
though some of the tattooing was clearly an amateur's work,
executed with a wavering hand. "How much you have suffered," he said softly, kissing Zoe's back, "—these needles
must have hurt." "*She* is there to be hurt," Zoe said contemptuously. Tristram closed his arms around the woman,
swaying over her. She was so much shorter than he! so much
smaller, as if belonging to another species! Rapid and glim-
mering the thought passed through his mind that, beneath
his superior weight, she would seem to be smaller still: and
that this would be part of the pleasure of her body.

He shuddered, and buried his face in her neck. Zoe squirmed free of him while not precisely repulsing him; she laughed, easing away, light on her feet as a dancer. Her ashy-brown hair, loosened, swung about her face; her cheeks were prettily flushed. Tristram dared not look upon the full length of her body; her splendid nakedness; fearing that the sharp-eyed young woman would see (but of course she *did* see) the desire in his face.

"My darling Fleur—"

"I am not she," Zoe said sharply. "I am I."

"Zoe—"

"I *am* Zoe: look at me!"

"You are so beautiful, even—"

"Even as I am disfigured? Say it!"

But Tristram could not look. He wiped his forehead with a handkerchief; blinking, and frowning; and said, in a nearly normal voice, as if they had been engaged in a conversation of an ordinary, if spirited, kind, "Tell me, please, if you can, Zoe, why did Fleur stay with Grunwald for so many years? —or, having stayed with him that long, why did she decide to flee when she did?"

Zoe's answer was direct, and derisory. "Because Grunwald threatened to do at last what, for a very long time, he had hinted, in jest, of greatly wanting to do."

"Which was—?"

"*Is.* For Grunwald means to do it now, when the little fool returns to him."

"*When* she returns—? You can't mean that you—that Fleur—will go back to Grunwald, after all this?"

"She will. I know. This flight, this 'break' for freedom, is short-lived. He will discover her here, and bring her back home. And, out of sheer cowardice, and terror, she will consent."

"Consent to return again, to that horror?"

"To her it is scarcely horror, but her life," Zoe said imperturbably. "At its worst the 'charming,' as Grunwald calls it, makes her cry out in pain,—she is a physical coward too: most pretty women are—but for the most part her ordeal is mild discomfort, a malaise kept hidden inside her expensive clothes and fey, silly, 'ladylike' demeanor. She will, in time, I predict, find salvation in God the Father; who, with all His faults, will not 'charm' her while she lives a mortal existence.''

" 'Charm'—?''

"The inscribing of charms.''

"The tattoos are charms?''

"The tattoos contain charms.''

"What kind of charms?''

"Says He, 'I alone know the charm.' ''

"Is it magic? The occult? Is Grunwald some sort of devil-worshipper?''

Zoe shook her head and said, with a sneering smile, "That, Angus, you must ask him yourself.''

"The man is a sadist; the man is mad!''

"You must ask him yourself.''

"But what was it, that finally drove you—''

"Fleur.''

"—drove Fleur away?''

Zoe coiled herself into the cushioned chair again, closing her silken robe carelessly about her. Her legs were exposed to the thigh, and beyond; beautifully shaped, rather long in proportion to her body, they too were covered with the eerie anquine designs. In the soft lamplight a kaleidoscope of colors gleamed, like jewels; rich carmines, emerald-greens, golds, purples, blues of many shades. . . . The tiny eyes winked, and stared; stared, it seemed, at Tristram, who stood as if under an enchantment. Since Zoe, insolent and suggestive in her smile, as in her posture, seemed to force him to it, he repeated his question: "But what was it that finally drove her away?''

" 'For chastity's sake,' says He.''

"Yes?''

" 'To purify, to purge, to extirpate,' says He.''

"Yes? What?''

"With his favored surgical instruments: 'Instruments of sanctity.' ''

"But what?"

Zoe beckoned to him. "Zoe will whisper in your ear. Zoe too would blush, were she obliged to say such things aloud."

Tristram bent over her, his breath warm and quick. He felt her arms close about his neck, as in the most delightful of dreams; he laughed in sheer startled pleasure and arousal, as Zoe tongued his ear. How could he bear it! He could not bear it!

Zoe then whispered her secret in his ear and he froze in horror. So quaint was the woman's language, so circumspect, he did not at first understand; or did not at first wish to understand. He swayed over her, sickened. "I have never heard of such a thing," he said. "I have never—heard of such a thing."

Zoe gave him an impatient little nudge, pushing him away as one might an animal, without precisely repulsing it. "Have you not?" she said coyly. "Then ask *him*. Gain admittance to Master's cave, and ask *him*."

Tristram's face was burning. "The man is mad. You—she—must never return to him; never so much as speak with him again. Grunwald is a monster and will have to be dealt with by the law."

Zoe made a show of yawning, showing her shadowy armpits. In her mock singsong she said, " 'I am Law. I am all that is.' "

"Grunwald is not above the law!"

" 'I am Law. I am all that is.' "

"We'll see about that. The bastard."

Zoe laughed. "Who has spoken?"

"—The man must die."

She drew the robe closer about her, as if chilled. "Who has spoken?" she repeated, more urgently.

"I have spoken."

"And 'I' is—?"

Tristram scarcely hesitated. "Angus Markham."

"And 'I' is brave enough, strong enough, hard enough, for such a task?"

Zoe spoke doubtfully; yet hopefully. She was lying in the chair with her head at a slant, observing Tristram along the curve of her cheekbones. Again she beckoned him to her and again Tristram knelt before her, trembling with desire, gathering her in his arms (how small she was! how slight! how easily subdued!) and covering her face, her eyes, her neck, her bosom, with ravenous kisses. Her arms closed tight about his neck; the sensation ran through him like a wave. She murmured, "Says He, 'I name love.'"

Tristram half shut his eyes, feeling he might faint. He said, softly, "Love."

He kissed Zoe's moist parted lips; pressed his eager weight against her; and Zoe arched herself against him, as if overcome suddenly with his very desire. Then, to Tristram's horror, she cried out sharply, in pain. "Oh! Angus! The needle has left me too raw—"

"The needle?"

"*His* needle," Zoe said, wincing. She examined with her fingertips, and gently rubbed, a tender reddened area on her belly, extending into the ashy-golden halo of pubic hair below, where the tattooing—lines of cuneiform verse in fierce orange ink—appeared to be fresh. The ink glowed as if incandescent.

"The monster's most recent 'charm,' done only last week!"

Tristram, by this time both weak with desire and wildly energized by it, did not know what to do. The blood beat hot in his face, and in his penis, which was stiff to the point of pain; swollen near to bursting. He told himself, You must not force your lust upon the poor woman . . . you must not.

So he stood, and adjusted his clothing, and made an effort to speak calmly. "Will you allow me to take you to a doctor?"

Zoe shook her head without seeming to hear. She examined the tattoo, poking her flesh rather rudely, impatiently. She said bitterly, "It has not healed. How he would laugh at me now, at me, and at you, seeing us, now!"

She stood, and closed the robe about her; weeping angrily; saying, "It has not healed. It has not healed. I was certain it had healed *and it has not.*"

Tristram said, "I love you, Zoe. I would do anything for you. Let me take you, now, to a—"

"Go away! You must go away, now! If you love me,—if you love her—you must go away now, before *she* returns. Pain and self-pity will bring her back; she is always close by, waiting; I feel her returning even now; poor piteous doomed woman! You must leave, Angus, if you love me, before *she* undoes all that we have done; and sends you away forever."

Before Tristram could protest, Zoe ran from the room; and Tristram was left alone. The fire burned behind him in the marble fireplace; out on Delancy Street, a single automobile passed quietly. Tristram whispered aloud, "It is not to be believed." He saw something gleaming on the carpet, and went to pick it up; an old-fashioned mother-of-pearl comb, shaped like a bow.

He turned the comb in his fingers and whispered, like a man under a spell, "It *is* to be believed."

III

1 Tristram left Delancy Street in a trance of oblivion; yet charged with purpose. For he knew now why he had come to Philadelphia: to kill a man named Otto Grunwald, a stranger to him; and to bring back with him, to Richmond, to his ancestral home, a beautiful young woman named Fleur Grunwald . . . Fleur, or Zoe . . . who was scarcely more than a stranger to him too.

Now I know my destiny, Tristram thought, impassioned. Now I know why I was born.

That night, he walked for hours; scarcely knowing where he was; bombarded with thoughts, plans, flashes of dream-like scenes,—rehearsals of the moment when he would raise his hand against Grunwald and strike him down. Would he use a knife? (He had no knife.) Would he use a gun? (He had no gun.) Perhaps, overcome with fury and loathing of his enemy, he would simply use his hands . . . his strong hands. (Tristram flexed his fingers and examined them in surprise. The fingers *were* strong; stronger than he recalled. Their backs were covered with white-blond hairs and the knuckles seemed enlarged. These were hands certainly capable of choking another man to death, and of taking pleasure in it!)

Tristram regretted for the moment that he was not home in Richmond since, there, it would be no difficult task to poke about in his father's things; the things his father had willed him; fishing and hunting knives . . . rifles . . . shotguns . . . several collector's handguns, including a German luger in working condition, souvenir of the War.

Like most of the male Heades, Tristram's father had been
a sportsman of a kind, with a gentlemanly and seasonal interest in killing wild creatures; he had strongly encouraged
Tristram to accompany him to the family hunting camp in
the Monongahela mountains, but Tristram had always de-
murred. Now, for the first time in his life, Tristram regretted
his solitary, bookish boyhood. I might have been baptized
in blood, he thought. My forehead dampened with blood
from my first deer kill.

The thought made him shudder.

And yet: wasn't it easily done? For after all it is done
all the time. Glancing through the Philadelphia newspaper
delivered to his hotel room, Tristram had been appalled
by the number of local crimes recorded. Most of the ar-
ticles were brief, no more than a paragraph or two beneath
a laconic headline, buried in the interior of the paper
amidst advertisements for women's fashions and lingerie:
gunman shoots down victims in street . . . husband kills
estranged wife, four-year-old child, and himself . . . drug-
dealers executed "gangland style" . . . six "badly decomposed" corpses, of indeterminate sex, discovered in
tenement apartment in South Philadelphia. There was a
spirit of madness in the very air perhaps!

Of course, Tristram's "crime" would be no crime at all
in the usual sense of the word, and he did not consider it
such. It would be a purely disinterested act of justice and
necessity: the monster-madman Grunwald must die that
lovely Fleur might live. So simple an equation as that.

Tristram seemed to know too that he would never be
caught. The very concept of being "caught" for so selfless
a deed was unthinkable; even vulgar. I will kill the man before he knows who I am, and what my purpose is, he
thought, excited. Blood pulsed through his body like the
fierce hot purposeful blood of carnal desire. For the first
time in his life Tristram understood why men died for love.
When he thought of poor Fleur . . . poor Zoe . . . her lovely
body disfigured as it was . . . and the threat of an unspeakable disfigurement, indeed mutilation, to come . . . he was

overcome with rage. *The man must die. The man must die. The man must die.* To throw one's life away in the service of love did not seem to him so extreme . . . though, prior to this, it had to be confessed that Tristram had encountered the motive only in books. He wondered if he had spent his youth collecting books, perusing them with an almost religious awe, in order that, one day, in the prime of his manhood, he would realize himself as a living breathing human being *with the motive, the passion, and the zeal* of an imagined being, whom love for a woman inhabited like a Fury of antiquity.

"How happy I am!"

He looked up startled to see the facade of the Hotel Moreau, its marquee still lighted though it was dawn; a splendid fresh golden-glowing dawn; the newly budded trees in the Square illuminated with light and moisture, like a nimbus surrounding the entire park. Had he walked all night? Where had he walked? The uniformed doorman hurried to open the door for him, murmuring, "Good morning Mr. Markham," and Tristram nodded, smiling, in reply. He would sleep; he would gather his strength; and, sometime within the next forty-eight hours,—he would give himself two days, which seemed more reasonable than merely one—he would murder Otto Grunwald.

2 Tristram slept; slept for six hours; so deep, profound, and wonderfully restorative a sleep, that, waking, he could scarcely remember where he was; or why.

Only that he had come a long distance; and had a very long distance to go.

Lying abed in his paralysis of sleep, as one struck dumb, or enchanted, he had heard the telephone ringing but had made no move to answer it; and eventually of course it had stopped ringing. Had it been Fleur? Markham himself? Someone from his past life?

"But no one must interrupt me now."

Tristram did not think it strange but, in its way, utterly natural, blessed as he was by Fleur Grunwald's love, that he seemed to have wakened with the outline of a strategy in his head; not a fully realized plan, for the details would have to be worked out *in medias res*, but a plan with which to begin. One of the antiquarian dealers with whom he had spoken the day before had mentioned that Otto Grunwald too was a collector: less of rare books and manuscripts than of antiquarian medical paraphernalia—including, coincidentally, yet, it almost seemed, naturally, ophthalmic prostheses, or *glass eyes*.

Tristram considered: as a riding horse has a "good" and a "bad" side by which he is approached so a man has a "good" and a "bad" side, and Tristram Heade, well versed in the obsessions of collectors, had no doubt but that he knew what Grunwald's "good" side might be.

Though it was not an easy task to speak with Otto Grun-

wald in person, nor even to locate a number by which the
millionaire philanthropist might be reached, Tristram
shrewdly persisted through a dozen or more telephone calls.
(As he ate, with distracted pleasure, but pleasure nonetheless, a lavish breakfast of eggs Benedict, Canadian bacon
crisply fried, strawberries, honeydew melon, and blueberries
topped with cream, elegantly presented by room service.)
First, he called the antiquarian dealer, who claimed not to
have Grunwald's private number; the man communicated
with his customer solely by mail, he said, sending brochures
and the like to Grunwald's office in the city. Several other
dealers, whom Tristram called next, told him the same
thing. He then called his lawyer cousin, who seemed surprised to hear Tristram's voice so soon again, though the
man was genial enough in explaining, with regret, that,
though the firm surely had Grunwald's private number
listed somewhere, he really could not give it out, "even to
a blood relative—even for a very good reason." Tristram
said quietly, "This is a slap in the face," and hung up before
his cousin could reply.

Next, though guessing it hopeless, he called one of the
numbers listed for Grunwald & Sons, Inc., and was told by
a motherly sounding receptionist, that, if the situation was
really "a sort of emergency" as Tristram said, he might send
a telegram to Mr. Grunwald's home on Burlingham Boulevard, with the request that Mr. Grunwald respond.

"Of course," Tristram said. "The very thing."

So excited was he, so inspired, the wording of the telegram came easily, even as he dialed Western Union to dic-
tate it. *Have precious collector's item belonging to you. Will
negotiate.* He hesitated over which name to use: Tristram, or
Markham. Fleur knew him as Markham, but did Grunwald
know Markham? Did he even know the name? Better to use
Tristram Heade, a name of absolute innocence, unsullied.
But for the telegram he would simply use his initials, and
ask Grunwald to telephone him here in the hotel *if interested.*

So confident was Tristram that Grunwald would respond,
that, being the man he was, Grunwald could not *not* re-

spond, he finished his breakfast in high spirits, and began his toilette in preparation for going out. As he shaved he whistled loudly, a cheery military tune, whose title he could not have named.

And the call, from a man who identified himself as Grunwald's personal secretary, did come, within the hour.

3

The appointment was set for 6:30 P.M. at Grunwald's home. It was now 3:15 P.M.

Tristram arranged for two dozen red roses to be sent to Fleur at Delancy Street, with the accompanying note: *My dearest darling, do not despair! I love you and I vow I will remove from your life any and all impediments to your happiness. When next you hear from me you may be a free woman. Your loving—*

He saw no alternative but to sign himself *Angus.*

(Thinking that, when he and Fleur were safely removed to Richmond, and to another, happier life, he would tell her who he really was.)

He then reread the note, and changed *may* for *will.* His fingers, gripping the pen, had begun to tremble.

Quite by chance, in a zippered compartment in Markham's suitcase which he had missed the other day, Tristram found, to his amazement, a sheathed dagger—a cruel-looking weapon with a ten-inch steel blade and a carved wooden handle.

Of course! The very thing!

He weighed it in his hand; stood before a mirror brandishing it; making short quick stabbing motions in the air; a bit awkwardly at first, then with more assurance. So I will not be forced to use my hands after all, he thought.

The dagger did not look new, yet its blade shone clean and razor-sharp. Tristram wondered to what purpose Angus Markham had employed it and his heart gave a little lurch of anticipation.

He also found, in the same compartment, a gold tie-clasp engraved with the initials *A T M*, a pair of gold cuff links, and three women's rings—a ruby, an opal, and a diamond-studded wedding band. The inside of the band was engraved *E S F.* "And what is one to make of all this?" Tristram wondered aloud. "Someday, perhaps, 'Angus' will explain."

In preparation for that evening Tristram tried on several outfits; settling finally upon a light tweed sports coat of Markham's, with leather elbow patches, that gave him, he thought, just the right air of the intellectual and the casual. He chose a white cotton shirt that might have been his own, and a necktie of alternating dark green and pale green stripes, very possibly his own. He regarded his mirrored reflection with guarded approval: a tall broad-shouldered handsome man with hair so pale as to appear white, a slightly flushed skin, and bright, hard, canny eyes, framed by rather scholarly glasses. An intelligent man, perhaps a university professor; certainly bookish; "sensitive"; a person of high integrity, not easily dissuaded from any mission. Extending his right hand to be shaken he said, smiling, "Hello. My name is—"

He sheathed the dagger without further examination, and slipped it into a pocket, where its bulge might be mistaken for a pipe, or a small book.

All the while, the glass eye was lying in the marble ashtray atop the dresser; unmoving; blind; yet staring, it almost seemed, in Tristram's direction. Tristram was uneasily aware of it, and did not neglect, before he left, to wrap it up carefully in a handkerchief, and place it in his inside breast pocket. "For safekeeping."

Time seemed to be passing with unnatural slowness, so Tristram decided to take a taxi to within a few miles of Grunwald's home, and walk, at his leisure, the remainder of the distance. Otherwise he feared he would find himself on

Delancy Street, staring up at *her* windows, like any lovelorn suitor.

You must not return to that woman empty-handed: your man's pride will not allow it.

Thus, strolling in Fairmount Park, on an embankment high above the Schuylkill River, Tristram thought of Fleur; and of Zoe; his thoughts oscillating helplessly between the two. He felt an almost unbearable tenderness . . . or did he feel desire so swift and violent it brought tears to his eyes. How sweet Fleur was, and how innocent!—how beautiful, how voluptuous, how seductive, Zoe! As in a vision Tristram saw again poor trembling Fleur in the doorway of his hotel room; as in a forbidden dream he felt again Zoe's arms around his neck and the surprising force of her lips against his . . . and, not least, her barbarously tattooed body. Of course, this body was Fleur's too. "I must keep that in mind."

Tristram checked his watch and discovered to his surprise that it was only 5:08 P.M. Was his watch working? He could not believe that time was passing with such excruciating slowness.

Surely it had been many hours since Grunwald's secretary had called?

But a passerby confirmed the time: in fact, the man's watch read 5:03.

So Tristram sat on a park bench beside a lagoon, to rest, and to wait; he was no more than a mile from Burlingham Boulevard, and did not want to waste his energy in purposeless tramping about, however attractive Fairmount Park. This was no pleasure outing after all: he had come to kill a man . . . a man whose name he had not known only a few days before . . . and whose face, even now, he did not know.

The curiosity of the situation rose before Tristram, suddenly. Had he not come to Philadelphia merely to buy two or three antiquarian books? Among them, Mr. Lux's "rare" folio edition of . . . whatever the title. It was a trip he had made numerous times, always by Pullman, and always, excepting the usual minor dislocations of travel, pleasurable. And now!

My dearest darling, do not despair, I will do anything anything anything for you I love you I adore you I vow to protect you with my life. . . . Tristram's fingers slipped inside his coat pocket, to touch, to caress, to confirm, Markham's splendid dagger.

But how would he use it? How, precisely?

The thought came to him that the most expeditious method of committing murder is probably, simply, to commit it; at an unexpected moment; at a moment, wayward-seeming, unpremeditated, when the agent himself (that is, the "murderer") does not expect to act. One gets into position; into what might be called the context of murder; and then,—"Taking yourself by surprise you take your quarry by surprise as well." Tristram shaped these remarkable words aloud though they were altogether new to him, so far as he knew.

Unless of course his father had passed this wisdom along to him, years ago, in Tristram's callow youth; when he had imagined himself immune to love, and to the consummation of manly honor.

"Excuse me, sir!"

Tristram glanced up to see before him on the path a white-haired old man in a panama hat and soiled, shabby clothing, a knapsack on his back and what appeared to be wires poking out of his collar; he blocked Tristram's way, smiling a kindly if strained smile, and extended for Tristram's perusal, or his purchase, a pamphlet titled in stark red letters *ARMAGEDDON: ARE YOU PREPARED? The Selected Wisdom of Bruno Love, Ph.D.*

Reared to be polite to any elder, Tristram was incapable of pushing rudely past the man, as others in the park had done; though indicating that he was in a hurry, with no time to spare, he could not forestall a small speech on the subject of Armageddon and the "harmonic concurrences of the universe," delivered in so brisk, clipped, and atonic a manner as to suggest a robot's voice. The old man's movements too were mechanical, as if he were wired; indeed, Tristram saw, amazed, he *was* wired; his panama hat seemed to be threaded with fine wires, and there was a network of wires visible inside his coat, like a spider's web. As the old man spoke in small rhythmic surges he blinked, and winked, and frowned, and smiled, and ceased to smile, and smiled again, and nodded, and extended the pamphlet another time, tapping Tristram's wrist with it, as if his speech were fully patterned in every respect, allowing no margin for error. He was a tall, spindly, dirt-encrusted old man who edged closer to Tristram than Tristram thought necessary, but his manner was eccentric rather more than threatening. "My name, sir, is Dr. Poins," he said, in his mechanical singsong, "—and there, sir, is Dr. Love. Dr. Bruno Love, Ph.D., my mentor of the past twenty-nine years, who chooses not to foist himself upon us."

There stood some yards away, off the path, a shy dwarf-sized oldish man; like Dr. Poins dressed in much-rumpled and soiled clothes, though not, like Dr. Poins, so far as Tristram could judge, wired. He could not have been more than four feet ten or eleven inches tall, with a nut-brown, slightly misshapen, yet rather sweet face; a look in his eyes, Tristram thought, of infinite sorrow, compassion, and wisdom. Something about him led Tristram to believe that he was mute; very likely, then, both deaf and mute. Yet he was standing, in the dreamy vitrescent light of late afternoon, in spring, in Fairmount Park, with a wonderful sort of dignity; even defiance.

As Dr. Poins continued to declaim of Armageddon, and the cosmic cycle of 166,666 years that was shortly to complete itself, Tristram, now rather desperate to be gone, took out his wallet, withdrew a bill, and pressed it into Poins's hand. He had noted that *ARMAGEDDON* was priced at fifty cents. "Sir, wait, oh sir, wait!" Poins said loudly, following after him, "—this is a five-dollar bill, sir, and I have no change,—you must know, sir, that a man like I, in my circumstances, sir, would not have change, in any case not the *correct* change, sir, no more than Dr. Love, who scorns all

material matter and mercenary gain, sir, and you have forgotten your pamphlet, sir, inadvertently insulting both Dr.
Love and I though you seem kind-hearted, sir, and mean
well! Yet do you suggest that I am to be pitied? That *Dr.
Love* of all persons is to be *pitied*? Is that your intent, sir,
or— Sir! I am addressing you! How dare you walk away!"

Poins, infuriated, limped along after Tristram like a small
yapping dog at his heels, shouting, and waving his arms in
scythelike mechanical gestures, drawing a good deal of
amused attention from passersby. "Sir! My curse upon you,
sir! To insult us, sir, when we bring such sinners as you
salvation! To insult Poins, sir, is human, but to insult Love,
sir, is the devil's work! My curse upon you, sir! May you
never forget this day or this hour!" Tristram, increasing his
stride, his face burning, called back over his shoulder that
he had meant to insult no one; he had no smaller change
than a five-dollar bill; he was in a hurry—"a desperate
hurry"—and could not stop to talk. Finally the old man
dropped back, panting, and winded, shaking a fist at Tristram; continuing to shout until Tristram was out of earshot.

What an absurd encounter! And at such a time! (It was
now 6:22 P.M.) Tristram descended a long sloping hill to
the street, stumbling, and nearly falling, his face very hot as
if he had indeed been guilty of insult, however inadvertent.
He had thought the white-haired old man a harmless eccentric. . . . And now he had drawn a curse upon his
head . . . at such a time.

He wondered what Markham would have done, in his
place. But Markham was doubtless too canny to ever find
himself in such a place.

4 Feeling rather self-conscious because he had come on foot, and not in a taxi, or, better yet, a limousine, Tristram rang a clapper-bell at the front entrance of the Grunwald estate, and was admitted, after a brief wait, by a grizzled black man in a uniform. Asked his name, he said, after a moment's hesitation, "Heade. Tristram Heade." He added, "I believe Mr. Grunwald is expecting me?" The black man regarded him with lustreless, unreadable eyes, and said, "If you are Heade, Tristram, as it's writ on this paper, yes, Mr. Grunwald is expecting you."

The Grunwald mansion was constructed of a darkish stone that drew in and seemed to absorb light; a stone that looked inordinately heavy, and solid. There was a high-peaked slate roof, there were numerous leaded windows, and, to one side, past which the black servant led Tristram, a pair of French doors leading onto a terrace ringed with evergreens in stylized sculpted shapes. A house in which no one lives, Tristram thought. He seemed to recognize the look.

Indeed, all of Burlingham Boulevard had this look. As of a sepia photograph, a daguerreotype, imprecisely reproduced. The sidewalks were unusually wide, but in poor condition; Tristram had been the sole pedestrian, and had had a sense, passing through Grunwald's neighborhood of mansion-sized houses, all of them set back from the street in impeccably tended lawns, of entering a depopulated world. The boulevard itself was empty; the tall plane trees that lined it had a melancholy autumnal look, as if their peeling bark meant death. The only visible activity was that of workmen of various kinds—gardeners, lawn crews, roofing repair men. In Grunwald's driveway, parked at the rear, and being hosed and polished, even now, by a black chauffeur, was a long sleekly handsome black Rolls-Royce.

Yet none of this, Tristram thought, will save the monster.

The black servant was leading Tristram along a dim-lit corridor whose walls were hung with oil portraits, presumably of Grunwald ancestors. Still heated from his encounter with the madman Poins, Tristram surreptitiously wiped at his face with a handkerchief; straightened his tie; pressed, with his right elbow, the dagger snug in his coat pocket. *Taking yourself by surprise you take your quarry by surprise as well.*

The black servant, about to open a door, glanced over his shoulder at Tristram, frowning. "Did you speak, sir?"

Tristram said, coolly, "I did not."

Otto Grunwald turned out to be so little like the man Tristram had anticipated, the first several minutes of their conversation passed in a sort of daze for him, while he blinked, and stared, and swallowed hard, and tried to get his bearings.

Grunwald was a man, clearly a gentleman, whom Tristram would have guessed to be in his early sixties; with a high, slightly pinched forehead, fair fine thinning silky gray hair, a narrow nose, narrow chin, "chiseled" lips. His eyes were of the color of damp stones, and sad; the left eye in particular. His skin was both fair, like Tristram's, and very faintly discolored, as if with a coppery or liverish undertone. Speaking, he chose his words with care and a look of distrust; his handshake had exuded a quick animation, quickly fading. Tristram thought: An ill man, who is determined to be well again.

They were seated in Grunwald's library, which reminded Tristram uneasily of his Grandfather Heade's library; though Grunwald, being a collector, as he called himself, of "variegated tastes," had amassed things that would have astonished Tristram's grandfather; including, most conspicuously, not one but two specimen skeletons from the London School of Medicine. " 'Adam' and 'Eve,' the medical students called them, though, to the layman's eye, they display no significant sexual distinction, save size. I must confess that I paid a fairly hefty price for them," Grunwald said, sighing, "—and I don't doubt that I was cheated. At the time, I was a very inexperienced collector, and my enthusiasm outran my perspicuity." Tristram nodded, and made a show, out of politeness, of examining the skeleton nearest him; the rather diminutive "Eve." The skull, eyeless, noseless, with many missing teeth, looked as if it might be made of papier mâché, inexpertly fashioned; the bones, blatantly wired as they were, and affixed to a metal pole, had a plasterish look, like a Hallowe'en decoration. How tragic our lives, Tristram thought, deeply moved, or are they merely farcical: to come, after so much passion, so much grief, so much joy, and doubtless many moments of pristine insight into the nature of one's fate, to *this*.

Grunwald said, with a confidential dip of his voice, "It does give me pleasure of a childish sort to 'see' my specimens through the eyes of a brother collector. One who can be expected to understand, and to sympathize." The lid of his right eye twitched as if in a wink.

Though Tristram's response was rather restrained, Grunwald went on to boast a bit of his collection of medical curiosities: on all of the walls were lithographs and engravings of medical scenes, depicting, among other things, early surgical operations in England, Germany, and Holland; there, in that glass-fronted cabinet, were rows of false teeth, the oldest dated 1723,—"hideous wooden chompers, aren't they"; in the adjacent cabinet, a display of antique syringes, hypodermic needles, and "douching" and "enema" devices,—"merely to look at them is to shudder, don't you think"; in other cabinets medical kits, blood-letting and surgical instruments, "leeching vials," and hearing-aid horns of various shapes and sizes. "The pride of my collection thus far is that kit of ophthalmic prostheses, or artificial eyes as they are called," Grunwald said, almost tenderly; but, as

Tristram merely frowned, and said nothing, the subject drifted by.

(On his feet, pacing about, gesturing, and smiling, and speaking at times rather exuberantly, Grunwald seemed to Tristram a fairly normal, even rather appealing person; yet with something stiff, even paralyzed, about his face. Had *he* an artificial eye? The left eye appeared to be fixed in its socket while the right moved easily. . . .)

The black servant reappeared, with drinks; Tristram found himself accepting a glass of rather too sweet Madeira wine; and talking, very nearly chatting, with Otto Grunwald, on the subject of collecting . . . which seemed to engage Grunwald so intensely, with such passion, Tristram could have been led to believe it was the purpose of their meeting. From time to time he paused, and said, "As I suggested in my telegram—" but Grunwald seemed not to hear, or, suddenly nervous, or distracted, murmured, "Ah, later,—there will be time for that later."

Tristram glanced at his watch. It was already 7:40 P.M.

Grunwald said, "It seems, Mr. Heade, that you and I have a party in common: the redoubtable Virgil Lux."

"Ah yes," Tristram said, blinking, "—Virgil Lux."

"He *is* a fine man, don't you think?"

"I think . . . I think he may now and then be duplicitous," Tristram said carefully.

"Do you really! Do you!" Grunwald leaned forward with such unfeigned interest, such a widening of his eyes, Tristram could not fail to be flattered.

There followed then an animated half-hour or more during which Grunwald plied Tristram with questions about Lux, and other Philadelphia dealers of Tristram's acquaintance, and Tristram answered, sometimes at length; all the while aware, or partly aware, that his meeting with Otto Grunwald was not developing along the lines he had anticipated. He had to forcibly remind himself, in the very midst of an amusing anecdote, that Grunwald was Fleur's husband . . . Zoe's husband . . . the man, the monster, who had held her virtually captive for years, and tattooed her lovely body in hideous serpentine designs . . . the likelihood of which, let alone the reality, here, in this elegant setting, with evidence on all sides of taste, discrimination, and care, seemed hard to grasp. He knew why he had come, and he was determined to fulfill his mission, and yet . . . *why* had he come, and *what* was his mission?

A voice counseled him: *Taking yourself by surprise you take your quarry by surprise as well.*

Ah yes.

And then it was 8:30 P.M. and a light rap at the door informed the gentlemen that dinner was served; and Tristram found himself, wine-warmed and somewhat sleepy, seated at a beautifully set table across from Otto Grunwald, and eating, with hapless pleasure, roast beef of exquisite tenderness; and drinking yet more wine. When, at last, toward the end of the meal, he said, "I am here, Mr. Grunwald, to represent your wife, who is deeply unhappy with—" Grunwald brushed the remark aside impatiently, and said, "I don't care to hear about my wife, Tristram—I hope I may call you Tristram?—or of the tales she spreads, of me, in this city. I am utterly, utterly sick of the subject; sick to the depths of my soul."

There was a moment's silence. Tristram stared at his host, quite astonished.

Grunwald continued, "This is a woman, Mr. Heade, whom I married out of love and idealism; and, though I should not want her to know it, pity. Yet within the space of a few years she has been unfaithful to me—I am certain of it. I do know that she has violated not one but several of the specifically itemized terms in our marriage contract; what is most shameful, and a source of unending sorrow to me, as to all the Grunwalds, is her insistence upon telling utterly fantastical tales of my alleged 'barbarism' and 'cruelty' to any and all who will listen. *The very same tales she told to me when we first met.*"

" 'Tales'?" Tristram asked weakly. " 'Fantastical'?"

Grunwald said with a bitter smile, "And Philadelphia is,

I hope I do not offend you with my language, a very cesspool of gossip. 'The more lurid, the more likely to be believed,' a society columnist for the *Inquirer* observed the other day, in print. She seemed to think it was a good thing.''

Tristram swallowed hard, and reached for his wineglass. His brow furrowed thoughtfully.

Grunwald said in a measured, reluctant voice, "I don't doubt that Fleur has appealed to your gallantry; you would not be the first man to have succumbed. She has cultivated a talent for enlisting others, including even certain female members of my family, in her campaign against me . . . her threat of causing scandal and bringing, as she says, 'infamy' upon my name, in the hope of getting a larger divorce settlement than the law would likely grant her. I am told that she has a lover, and will remarry at once, no matter how she denies it . . . a man she met at the racetrack at Saratoga . . . a stranger to me." He looked at Tristram, his right eye sharply in focus. "Is his name known to you?"

"No," Tristram said. "Certainly not."

"Of course, she would have sworn you to secrecy, in any case," Grunwald said. There was another brief pause. One set of plates was being cleared and another brought to the table. "Yet to my shame, Tristram, I must confess that even now I adore the woman, and would probably take her back at a moment's notice. And forgive her all her cruelty. She's so very beautiful, and has that air about her, when she's most herself, of supreme innocence!"

Tristram said, "I find it very difficult to believe, Mr. Grunwald, that—"

"It *is* difficult to believe," Grunwald said heatedly, "—in fact it is impossible to believe, the bizarre tales that woman spins. Her doctor tells me it is a symptom of her illness, and not a moral failing as such; that is, she does not *lie*; except as children of the ages of six, seven, eight, are said to lie, in inventing odd little fairy tale–like stories in which they themselves are the central characters, often the victims. Have you ever heard of such a thing?"

Tristram had heard of such a thing, in regard to young

children; but shook his head resolutely, no. He did not at all like the direction in which this conversation was moving.

Grunwald said, with an air of dreamy regret, "When I first met Fleur she was only seventeen years old . . . the foster child of the pastor of the church to which I belong. . . . I knew of her unhappy background, and, by degrees, she told me more . . . an alcoholic father who abused the family, and eventually disappeared; an emotionally unstable mother, also an alcoholic, who lived with a succession of 'husbands,' and made no effort to protect her daughter from them; an abusive older brother . . . whom she accused of 'sullying' her when she was eight years old. This brother, she claimed, was not only sexually exploitative but sadistically inclined; he tortured her by tying her up, holding lighted matches against her skin, even 'tattooing' her. (She showed me several of these 'tattoos' on her arms and upper body; I learned after we were married that they were merely designs she had painted on herself with vegetable dye! Yet she was oddly proud of them, and ashamed of them, *as if they were real.*) If only Fleur could have been an actress, she might have put her talent for duplicity to some use! But she lacks the seriousness, and the stamina. Professional acting is a very different matter from the sort of performances she gives."

"Tattoos? Vegetable dye?" Tristram asked, staring.

"Once, when she was ill with a fever, she raved about an infant she'd had . . . that had died at childbirth . . . or had somehow suffocated. She hinted that this infant was the result of an incestuous rape but of course I have no way of knowing if she spoke the truth, or even, in her state, if she knew the truth. She is supremely gifted at self-dramatization, as perhaps you know," Grunwald said, sighing, "yet, like you, I would probably believe her, still . . . to a degree, at least . . . if she comes back to me as she has in the past, repentant, yet insisting upon *her* innocence, and *my* cruelty."

"What did you say about tattoos?—and vegetable dye?" Tristram asked.

"I don't want to expose poor Fleur any further," Grunwald said. "If she and her attorney force the issue, we will have a day, many days in fact, in court; until then I had better remain silent. But you should know, Tristram, that this is not the first time Fleur has left me, nor is it likely to be the last. Unless she *does* have a lover, and he too forces the issue. . . . It has been her habit every eighteen months or so to run off, and hide with one or another indulgent female relative of mine (I don't doubt but that she is in Delancy Street at the moment but *I will not compromise you by asking*); then she returns, seemingly genuine in her repentance, though always claiming it was I who drove her off. Such a pretty, fickle, shallow creature!—and yet I adore her! What's to be done!"

Tristram stared at something gleaming and glittering on the table before him. He said, dully, "Yes. What's to be done."

"There *is* a sort of fairy-tale fatedness about her," Grunwald said. He spoke with the compulsiveness of the besotted lover, grateful for any audience. "One finds it in a certain type of woman, throughout history. Helen of Troy must be the archetypal figure . . . though it's said that the woman herself did not exist, but is only emblematic. Still, women like Fleur certainly exist; the sort of women that influence us so passionately, yet, it seems, unconsciously, we can't hope to fathom, let alone control, the power they release. They seem to make of us more manly men than we know ourselves . . . they arouse in us the desire to 'save' them . . . to shield them from their fates . . . even as, by their own design, *we* become their fates." Grunwald laughed helplessly. "It is all diabolical . . . it is the oldest of stories. You look, Tristram, as if you are pained by what you hear?"

Tristram's mouth felt uncomfortably tight. He said, "I was thinking, Mr. Grunwald, that, though you seem to grant a sort of power to your wife, she is, nonetheless, very frightened of you."

"*She is not frightened enough,*" Grunwald said quietly, rising from the table. He made an effort to smile. "Shall we adjourn to the other room, Tristram? And would you please call me Otto?"

They returned to Grunwald's library, to share a bottle of Portuguese liqueur, and two of Grunwald's enormous Havana cigars, which, after an initial shock as of a highly potent drug hitting his veins, Tristram found himself enjoying; though he had never smoked a cigarette in his life, still less a cigar. He supposed it was Markham's influence and he made a note to resist it, at another time.

There followed then a curious interlude during which Otto Grunwald, his patrician face rather flushed, showed Tristram some of the "printed treasures" of his collection. The material inside the locked glass case was old, for the most part; much of it beautifully bound; probably rare; probably very expensive; yet, to Tristram's discerning eye, indiscriminately gathered, arranged by mere subject matter and not language, period, publisher, or that elusive element known as quality. The collection constituted, as Grunwald rather passionately declared, "evidence *contra* Woman" which he had begun assembling in the mid-1950s, after the breakup of his first marriage. Books of varying sizes; elegant folio editions; pamphlets; crudely printed broadsides, caricatures, and cartoons, on the "natural inferiority" of the female sex: their wickedness, lasciviousness, duplicity, hypocrisy, impiety, cruelty, stupidity, vanity, sub-hu*man*ity. . . . "I keep this case under lock and key," he told Tristram in a lowered voice, "not wanting the servants, or *her*, to peruse it."

Despite himself Tristram was both revolted and fascinated. Grunwald's treasures *were* extreme: crudely executed anatomical drawings of women, whole and dissected . . . a series of elegant leatherbound engravings titled "The Burning of the Witches of Mora, 1670" . . . an illustrated edition of John Knox's *The First Blast of the Trumpet Against the Monstrous Regiment of Women* (1558) . . . misogynist broadsides, caricatures, cartoons . . . pornographic novels, illustrated . . . and in their midst handsomely bound editions of Ca-

tullus, St. Augustine, St. Thomas Aquinas, Martin Luther . . .
*A History of Christianity, Judaism, and the Pagan World . . . The
Wisdom of St. Paul* . . . Swift's *Gulliver's Travels* . . . Schopen-
hauer's *The World as Will and Idea* . . . *Le Diable, Erotologie de
Satan* (Paris, 1861) . . . Strindberg's *Marrying* and *The
Father* . . . treatises on medieval witches and witchcraft . . .
A *Manual of Lunacy in Females* (London, 1854) . . . *Debilitat-
ing Diseases of the Female Organs, Their Causation and Surgical
Cure* (London, 1883) . . . *Obscure Diseases of the Brain, the
Mind, and the Womb* (London, 1898) . . . *The Causation,
Course, and Treatment of Moral Insanity in Women* (London,
1900) . . . *Climacteric Derangements of Females* (London,
1903) . . . *A Handbook of Uterine Therapeutics and of Diseases
of Women* (Boston, 1909) . . . *What Little Sadie Saw; and How
She Regretted It* . . . *A Manual for Men Only* . . . *Whips, Straps
& Studs* . . . *Witches of the Modern Era, Their Detection & Purg-
ing* . . . *The Illustrated Jack the Ripper* . . . *The Illustrated Gilles
de Rais* . . . *The Illustrated Marquis de Sade* . . . *Les Amours
étranges* . . . *Les Agents de Lucifer* . . . *Cannibalism and Human
Sacrifice Through the Ages: With 101 Illustrations* . . . *The Drawings of Aubrey Beardsley* . . . *The Art of the Tattoo* . . . *What
Ingeborg Saw, and How She Regretted It* . . . *The Aryan Destiny:
Illustrated* . . . *The Mark of the Beast: Detection & Delectation* . . .
Hysteria: Detection and Curative Practice. . . . Mistaking Tristram's expression for one of intense interest, if not sympathy, Grunwald said, "I'm afraid my treasures do require
sorting and cataloguing. In the white heat of acquisition,
such details are often neglected. Ah, but here: here is the
very heart of the collection!—though no one would ever
guess, I am certain."

He withdrew one of the handsome leatherbound books,
a Victorian edition of Tennyson's *Idylls of the King,* saying,
as he opened it to a much-consulted page, "You know, I
assume, the scene in which Merlin explains the source of
his magical powers to Vivien . . . ? It is a book, itself; an
ancient volume whose 'every square inch has an awful
charm.' *Writ in a language that has long gone by . . . /And every
margin scribbled, crost, and cramm'd/ With comment, densest con-*

densation, hard . . . /And none can read the text, not even I:/ *And none can read the comment but myself;/ And in the comment did I find the charm*. There, do you see: *in the comment did I find the charm*."

" 'Charm'?" Tristram asked.

"The 'charm' is a spell of power used by an ancient king to subordinate a proud, headstrong, rebellious queen," Grunwald said. "He charmed her, the poet says—*In such-wise that no man could see her more,/ Nor saw she save the king, who wrought the charm,/ Coming and going, and she lay as dead,/ And lost all use of life.*" He looked up at Tristram in triumph. "You see? We have the power of the 'charm,' if we are but bold enough, manly enough, to seize it."

" 'Charm'—?"

Tristram stared at the page Grunwald was holding up to him, but could not read a word of the verse; the ornate typeface swam in his vision. "It rests with us, to seize the power of the charm," Grunwald said excitedly. "To make of their enslavement of us *their* enslavement. Do you see?"

"I—"

"It is *their* power against *ours*; a fight to the death, if necessary," Grunwald said. " 'And damn'd be he who first cries *Hold*'!"

"I'm not sure that I—"

"Have you ever been married?"

"No."

"Have you ever been in love?"

Tristram hesitated only a moment. "Yes. But I—"

"Then you have been, or will shortly be, betrayed," Grunwald said, shutting up the book, and returning it to its place on the shelf. "It is only a matter of time, my friend. Though you may delude yourself otherwise."

Grunwald locked the glass case, and slipped the key into his pocket. His right eye was brimming with moisture.

Tristram drew breath to speak, to protest, but Grunwald continued, with a grim smile, "As I, and numberless others, from the time of Adam to the present hour, have deluded ourselves. In the name of the loftiest of ideals—*Love*."

Was Otto Grunwald mad?—or had the man in his possession, *as if it were fated*, a special wisdom, of which Tristram Heade had never guessed?

Tristram stood tall, clumsy, baffled; his face burning; a roaring in his ears as of voices, distant and teasing. He had come to Grunwald's house on a mission he could not quite recall except to know that it was indeed a mission . . . and must not casually be abandoned. At the back of everything was Fleur's tearstreaked face; and Zoe's tearstreaked face; and . . . another face, resembling his, yet not his, and not known to him. *You fool, what are you doing! How have you allowed yourself to succumb to the enemy!*

Grunwald was asking would Tristram like a little more liqueur; and would he like to see more of the collection? For the hour after all was still young.

Though Tristram did not recall saying yes, he soon found himself with his liqueur glass in hand, replenished; and his cigar, which had gone out in an ashtray, relighted. Otto Grunwald, now more relaxed, and clearly enjoying himself, opened another of the glass cases, and showed Tristram his assemblage of medical instruments, primarily English, but also Dutch, German, and Belgian, of the mid- and late nineteenth-century. "Frightful instruments, aren't they?" he said, shivering. "Ah, the size of this hypodermic! Can you imagine! And this catheter! Of course, they knew no better in those days; physicians no less than doctors. —This was a leeching vial: you know, I suppose, what leeches were?—*are?*"

Tristram nodded, staring.

"And these are scalpels, with their several blades that fit inside them, do you see?—like this."

Tristram shyly lifted one of the instruments, and laid it down again.

"I am not sure of the use of this ugly little scoop, but this queerly shaped pair of pliers was used for pelvic examinations, I was told. On female patients of course."

Tristram stared, biting hard on his cigar. "Of course."

"These instruments here, in this black velvet case," Grunwald said, "—I have the word of my London dealer that they were used by the renowned Dr. Isaac Baker Brown, the Englishman who was first something of a vogue and then, I'm afraid, something of a martyr, in the late 1860s, when his colleagues expelled him from the Obstetrical Society, for his pioneering efforts in promoting sexual surgery in England. You are familiar with the tradition of clitoridectomy, Tristram, I suppose?"

" 'Clitoridectomy'—?"

"The removal of certain parts of the female genitalia, in the interests of health," Grunwald said.

" 'Health'—?"

Grunwald proceeded to describe, in detail, and with an unnerving enthusiasm, the clinical phenomenon of *clitoridectomy*, of which, in truth, Tristram had never heard. (Or *had* he heard of it, only recently?) At first, Tristram felt simple shock; then embarrassment; then a sort of diffuse shame; then, to his disgust, a sort of confused arousal. Grunwald concluded, "There are women in our midst who are, in a sense, freaks of nature; monsters of strength, egotism, wickedness, purpose, and, most absurdly, physical appetite; *women very like men, in short.* But it has always been within man's power to modify . . . to excise . . . to purge . . . the physical basis of their unruly nature, by way of surgical intervention. In this, we have historical precedence in most of the countries of the world."

Tristram frowned, and could not think of a reply.

After an awkward pause Grunwald said casually, "Of course, the procedure has been officially outlawed, for some decades, in the so-called civilized nations. It has been argued in certain quarters to be . . . barbaric."

Grunwald closed the cabinet, and locked it; and, next, led Tristram to an examination of "Adam" and "Eve," of whom, since returning to Grunwald's study, Tristram had been uneasily aware. (For the skeletons, though eyeless, nonetheless seemed to be watching the two men, with a certain ironic intensity.) With the flair of a medical lecturer, in whom awe for his subject and familiarity with it strangely contended, Grunwald spoke for a brief while of the skeletons, both in themselves, as *coups* of collecting, and generically, as specimens. Such terms as "interior maxillary," "humerus," "ulna," "scapula," "sacrum," "coccyx," "fibula" rolled off his tongue, leading Tristram to ask if he had ever studied medicine. Grunwald said, with a frowning smile, that, yes, he had *studied* medicine . . . but found the work not altogether to his taste. He had quit in his second year of medical school to take up responsibilities with the family business and had never regretted his decision; though, as he confessed, he felt himself inexplicably drawn to the discipline of medicine . . . to its atmosphere, its paraphernalia, the historic underpinnings of its practice. "I am a physician manqué, I suppose," Grunwald said, fondly stroking the discolored skull of the female skeleton, and poking a forefinger, in playful emphasis, into an eyeless socket. "*She* has doubtless complained to you, as to all the world that will tolerate her slander, of my overscrupulosity regarding her physical self . . . ?"

"To a degree," Tristram said guardedly.

Grunwald smiled at him, blinking. "You *are* here, are you not, on a mission of . . . what might be called 'mercy'?"

"I'm not altogether sure," Tristram said, "what it might be called."

Grunwald said wryly, "Ah, women are so capricious, aren't they! Yet so strong-willed! And they arouse, in us, a corresponding capriciousness, and strength!—for there is no other way to deal with them. It is a matter, you know,— as any horseman knows—of who will be master: the *rider*, or the *mount*. In nature, there is never any doubt; the weak succumb to the strong, and, should they wish to survive, must succumb intelligently, even, one might say, cunningly, to the strong. I do not require of any of my wives, and certainly not of little Fleur, that she acquiesce to me in everything; only that she acquiesce in those matters in which I am presumed to have knowledge. Even so," Grunwald said, fixing Tristram with an intense, radiant look, "I do not object to the claim of certain women for legal equality, under our Constitution, and for as much 'financial equality' as they can wrest from us, in the marketplace. I am a liberal, I hope, in such matters. But it is futile, as history demonstrates, for the sex to lay claim to moral and intellectual equality. In the areas of business, finance, politics, warfare . . . in medicine, law, science, mathematics . . . in invention . . . in music, art . . . architecture . . . literature . . . even in such presumably 'feminine' pursuits as cooking, and fashion design . . . one might say *in the very enterprise of civilization itself* . . . women's performance has been a sorry one. Of course they offer a multitude of excuses, pleading a history of *our* dominion; blaming Nature, even as they seek to argue that 'Nature' is not their destiny, and cannot circumscribe them. Certainly one encounters, from time to time, in the sex, rare individuals who seem to disprove the rule, by violating or transcending it; as one encounters, in our sex, rare individuals whose talents or idiosyncrasies mark them for special destinies. But what of it? Women *are* Nature, as Schopenhauer argues, the most seductive of traps, but traps nonetheless. Their capacity for the cultivation of physical life apart from reproduction and, at times, apart from *us*, is a hellish modern inclination that must be curtailed. Women are vessels for the solace of men's souls, and for men's pleasure; vehicles, you might say, for salvation—*theirs* and *ours*." Grunwald had been speaking rather passionately; he paused now, to wipe his mouth with a handkerchief. "I see by your expression, Tristram, that you do not quite agree—?"

Tristram stood frowning; feeling himself, more than ever, inordinately large and clumsy; very like a bear on its hind legs. He did not meet Grunwald's bright, impassioned gaze, as he said, "I—I do not quite know, Mr. Grunwald, whether I agree or—or do not agree."

"But I've asked you to call me 'Otto,' Tristram," Grunwald said warmly. "Can you not call me 'Otto'?"

" 'Otto.' "

"Yet with feeling, and not merely as an obligation?"

"*Otto.*"

"Ah, thank you! I am relieved that *she* has not poisoned you against me altogether, Tristram! *Very* relieved."

Grunwald clamped his hand on Tristram's shoulder, and led him, at last, away from the skeletons; in the direction of another locked glass-front cabinet, in which, on glass shelves, egg- or stone-shaped objects shone like jewels. Tristram felt both sick and excited; weakened, and aroused. He wondered what was happening to him . . . why he felt, in Grunwald's presence, so undefined, rudderless . . . *strange*. His resolve seemed to have drained from him completely; his strength, conviction, and will. Where, now, was Angus Markham's sharp, shrewd, canny voice? Where, the man's combative self? *His* center of gravity? It might have been the late hour, or the amount of alcohol Tristram had had to drink, or the cigar, or, yet more insidious, the powerful personality of his host, but Tristram had the idea that Markham had withdrawn from him, or was, at least temporarily, lost . . . as a radio station might grow weak, or fade away altogether, though the dial remains untouched.

Grunwald, unlocking the cabinet, said affably, "In a way these are the jewels of my collection. They have a personal significance to me . . . that goes beyond mere temperamental inclination."

"Glass eyes!" Tristram murmured.

"Yes," Grunwald said, "—and most of them are truly old-fashioned glass, or cryolite glass, not more modern-day specimens."

A cabinet of artificial eyes: arranged both collectively, in medical kits, and singly, on tiny cushions. Tristram stared, really quite amazed. The eye he'd found on the street . . . the eye now in his pocket . . . these eyes of which Otto Grunwald spoke so fervently. . . . What did it all mean? It could only be a coincidence, of course, but what did it mean?

"Few people notice, since, today, artificial eyes are so cleverly crafted, in plastic and whatnot," Grunwald was saying, "but I myself have an artificial eye: the left. Do you see?

Did you see?'' He gave the eye a light tap with his forefinger; not wanting to seem rude, Tristram professed surprise. "My eye was lost when I was ten, in an accident," Grunwald said, "but please don't feel sorry for me,—I've completely adjusted to life with one eye, as most people in my position do. For, after all," he said, smiling bravely, "as they say, the difference between two eyes and one eye, and one eye and no eye, is considerable."

Eye-making, Grunwald told Tristram, had been a precision craft for centuries. The first artisans made eyes for idols and statues, as long ago as 500 B.C., in Egypt; it was in the eighteenth century that their use, for men, was extensively developed. "These curious little beauties here," Grunwald said, indicating, but not touching, several extremely artificial-looking eyes on cushions, "date from about 1750, and are Dutch. Really quite priceless today." More plentiful were cryolite eyes of the nineteenth century, which comprised most of Grunwald's collection; these were first developed in 1835 by the German dollmaker Ludwig Muller-Uri, who used them, of course, initially, for his dolls. "This sort of glass—here are several excellent specimens, on this shelf—is a very hard but light substance that gives the eyes an accurate whitish-gray sclera tone. For the human eyeball after all is not really white, as the 'white' race is hardly white. The color comes from combining cryolite glass with arsenic oxide to provide sodium aluminum fluoride. Aren't they fascinating! One wonders to whom they belonged, into whose eyeless sockets they were once encased! —These eyes, nearly as lifelike, are made of vulcanite, and date from about 1869; these are of celluloid, and date from about that time. I am told they are Belgian. And these beautiful specimens, this entire shelf in fact, were crafted by James T. Davis, an American, one of the greatest craftsmen in the history of eye-making. But I don't suppose you will have heard of him. . . . What is it you have *there*?"

Wordlessly, guided by a sort of dim impulse, Tristram had removed the artificial eye from his pocket, and held it out for his host to see. It was very like several of the eyes in

Grunwald's collection, even to the tawny-brown-blue color of its iris.

Grunwald said incredulously, "But it is *my eye!* One of my Muller-Uri eyes, stolen from this very cabinet a dozen years ago!"

Tristram said, "*Your* eye?"

"Is this what you meant by your telegram? When I had thought you were referring to—another matter?" Grunwald asked, astonished. He had taken the eye out of Tristram's hand and was now examining it in the lamplight. "It is definitely my eye," he said, staring at Tristram suspiciously. "How on earth did you come by it?"

"I found it," he said defensively, "on a Philadelphia street."

"*Found* it? On a street? When?"

"Just the other day."

"The other day? After so many years?"

"Am I being interrogated?" Tristram asked, managing a stiff smile. "As I said, I found it on a Philadelphia street; I have forgotten the name. It was lying on the pavement, and I picked it up and put it in my pocket. By the oddest of coincidences—"

Grunwald interrupted excitedly. "But how did you know it was mine?"

Tristram's face flushed. He did not like Grunwald's peremptory tone. "I don't really know it *is* your eye, Mr. Grunwald, do I?"

Grunwald said, "Of course it's mine. It was reported stolen to the Philadelphia police, in 1966, along with a number of other items. I have the original bill of sale, from a London dealer; and, in any case, who else in Philadelphia would such a collector's item belong to? Have you brought it here to sell it back to me? To exact a sort of ransom?" He stared at Tristram as if Tristram were indeed a thief; in a matter of seconds the camaraderie between them seemed to have entirely vanished.

Tristram said, with dignity, "Certainly not."

"Ah, but in your telegram—"

"I wasn't referring to—"

"—you spoke of a collector's item—"

"You know what—*whom*—I was referring to."

Grunwald, breathing harshly, said, "Tell me, then: did you, or *she*, compose the message?"

Tristram said stiffly, "I composed it myself."

"Under whose influence, may I ask?"

Grunwald had placed the artificial eye atop his desk, where it gleamed and glittered in the lamplight, like a living eye; there was a subtle horror in its flattened sphere, and the bright acuity of its tawny-brown-blue iris. It is watching us, Tristram thought,—it will be a witness. The men quarreled about the telegram; and about Fleur; and about the ownership of the eye; Grunwald went to his filing cabinet, and produced a bill of sale from a London dealer, dated August 20, 1956, describing a cryolite eye, from the workshop of Muller-Uri, which he had purchased that day; and Tristram said stubbornly that the bill of sale did not prove the eye purchased was in fact the eye on the desk; and Grunwald, now quite agitated, but making an effort to speak calmly, said that, if Tristram insisted, they could consult a specialist who would make the identification. And they could call the police: for it was a matter after all of *stolen goods.*

Tristram said that he did not acknowledge any fact of "stolen goods"; so far as he was concerned, the eye was his, since he had, merely by chance, found it on the street; and had, merely by chance, brought it along tonight, to show to Grunwald. Grunwald stared at Tristram as if he thought him mad; shook his head; seated himself behind his desk, wearily, with the air of an old man, and pressed his hands against his eyes in a gesture of such bafflement, and fatigue, that Tristram felt his heart soften . . . for he quite understood the ardor of a collector for one of his prized items. And he thought, *I* do not really want the glass eye; why have I become so belligerent all of a sudden?

After a long, pained moment, Grunwald peered at Tristram through his fingers, his right eye bloodshot and damp with moisture. He said, in a subdued voice, "I seem to have forgotten that of course there was a reward for the return of the eye. There *is* a reward, extant. A negotiable reward. . . . In my surprise and . . . upset . . . I seem to have forgotten my good sense. This business with my wife has affected me terribly but of course that is no excuse. If you would allow me to . . ."

Tristram said quickly, "Not at all, Mr. Grunwald. Please accept the eye. I have no use for it, I am not a collector along those lines, I quite sympathize with your predicament, and I am sorry that . . ."

"Thank you so much! Thank you enormously!"

The words came out in a whisper. For a moment Grunwald looked as if he might cry in sheer gratitude; or was his expression, Tristram thought, one of greed, and incredulity that that greed was to be satisfied . . . ?

He wiped his face with his handkerchief, and said, smiling a strained smile up at Tristram, who loomed very tall over him, "But won't you allow me to give you something? An honorarium of a kind?"

"Not at all, Mr. Grunwald," Tristram repeated.

Grunwald fell to contemplating the eye, framing it reverently with his hands as if it were a rare, exquisite jewel. "Ah, how beautiful it is! And how extraordinary, that it should be returned to me, after so many years!" He beckoned Tristram to come closer, and Tristram did so, leaning over the desk, and staring at the gleaming object which both was, and was not, a recognizably "human" eye; his gaze drifting to the top of Grunwald's head . . . an altogether handsome, even noble head . . . with silvery-fine hair, thinning at the crown so that one could see the pink-toned vulnerable scalp beneath. As Grunwald hunched forward, the collar of his velvet smoking jacket pulled back, to expose his neck; a pale, finely-creased, but quite solid neck, upon which small curls and wisps of hair grew, of a generally darker hue than the rest. "Do you see how cleverly the artist has simulated the 'ambituity' of the iris?" Grunwald asked, as much of himself as of Tristram. He indicated, but did not touch, the glittering glass. "How extraordinary it is, and what a coincidence, that all *this* has come about. . . ." With the ease of an actor who has played his role countless times, so that the "artificial" has become transmogrified into the "natural," Tristram reached in the right-hand pocket of his coat, and—

At that moment there was a loud knocking at the door. And Grunwald looked up startled; and Tristram quickly stepped aside; and whatever was to be, was not, at least at that moment, to be.

5 "This is my nephew Hans," Grunwald said, making an effort to speak genially, "—and this, Hans, is Tristram Heade, a fellow collector—"

"Hello, how d'you do," Hans said, his words so perfunctory, and his handshake so minimal, Tristram might, in other circumstances, have felt slighted. But Grunwald's nephew—nearly as tall as Tristram, and big-shouldered, with a head of reddish curly hair that looked oiled, and a little-boy face both angelic and pouting—was not a young man from whom one might reasonably expect courtesy; his rudeness was simply part of his manner, like his rapid, dazzling, immediately fading dimpled smile, and the well-practiced level gaze of his brown eyes. A man attractive to women, Tristram thought. In his younger days, in Virginia, Tristram had so frequently encountered such men— spoiled, vain, "charismatic"—capable of extraordinary acts of derring-do and courage (as in a football game: for such men were often football players in college) and capable of extraordinary acts of callowness and cruelty (as in their dealings with women, or men judged as weak)—that he had acquired a social manner with which to deal with them: simply to say very little, and to step aside as soon as the protocol of handshaking was finished. For, beyond a quick, instinctive assessment of Tristram's probable physical prowess, and that quiddity understood as "masculinity," such men had very little interest in him. He was of course big; and surely strong; but there was the matter of his face, his eyes, his characteristic "sensitive" expression. . . .

Tonight, however, for a prolonged moment, Hans Grun-wald did stare at Tristram; almost, to Tristram's distress, as if he knew him. The brown eyes narrowed; the mouth twitched; then Hans looked away, and did not so much as glance at Tristram again, as if Tristram had ceased to exist. If he had troubled to note the artificial eye on Grunwald's desk he had as unthinkingly, if not contemptuously, dis-missed it too.

Grunwald was on his feet, demanding of his nephew with surprising anger why he had come, at this hour, uninvited, to disturb the peace of the house, and to talk of a matter both of them knew to be closed.

Sullenly, Hans said that he'd come because he had no choice: "You don't return my telephone calls, Uncle." His lips twisted about the word "uncle" as if it were a playful sort of obscenity.

Tristram quickly offered to leave the men alone together, since the hour *was* late; but Grunwald would not hear of it. "Hans and I will have our conversation elsewhere, and briefly," he said, taking the young man by the arm, and almost forcibly leading him from the room.

Grunwald's nephew was half a head taller than Grun-wald, and far more muscular, but he obeyed with the alacrity of a certain sort of killer-dog, who needs only to be taken in hand by his master to be restrained.

At least, Tristram thought, for the moment.

They quarreled in the hall, then in an adjacent room, a dispute over money, Tristram gathered; the words *gambling, loan, interest rate, debts, allowance, insubordination* penetrated the wall. At least at the start of the argument the elder man's voice was the louder; Tristram could only hear the low, muf-fled, furious sound of Hans's voice, not individual words.

Alone in Grunwald's study! The prospect was enormously exciting, as if, without quite knowing it, Tristram had been waiting for this moment all evening.

(He was still quite heated from the exchange over the artificial eye; his heartbeat remained pleasurably fast. That

moment when Grunwald had sat at his desk, and framed
the eye with his hand, and leaned forward . . . what an
exquisite moment that had been! Tristram's fingers had
moved of their own volition to his pocket, to the handle of
Markham's dagger, and the command *Strike, strike, strike!*
had rung in his ears.)

Of course there was no time now for Tristram to search
the room, or the house, but, acting quickly, and boldly, he
went to one of the several windows in the room and, using
Markham's knife, in quick, unhesitating, practiced strokes,
cut through the burglar-alarm wire. This had the effect—
startling but not surprising—of tripping the burglar alarm;
and causing a good deal of noise. Tristram thought, There.
That's done.

For though the household was, for a few minutes, in an
upset, the apparent cause of the alarm—Tristram having
innocently opened a window—was quickly detected; and the
alarm system turned off. Tristram apologized to Grunwald,
saying that he'd simply wanted some fresh air, and Grunwald, whose good eye was now quite threaded with blood,
and a very poor match for its healthier-appearing mate, said
irritably, "Of course it's nothing, please don't concern yourself, the wretched 'security system' goes off all the time, I
am sick to death of it and would just as soon dismantle it
permanently." He gazed at Tristram as at an old friend
whose name he could not recall, and excused himself another time, saying that he and his nephew had not yet finished their conversation.

Tristram, feeling wonderfully emboldened,—for one
unit of success always stirs in us the energy, no less than the
will, for another—this time put himself in a position to
eavesdrop. The men were in a room immediately to the left;
Tristram simply tiptoed along the corridor, his head inclined, until he stood at the closed door, where the men's
voices were quite audible. If the black butler discovered him
he would invent on the spot some sort of excuse, but the
black butler did not discover him, nor did Grunwald and

his nephew, embattled as they were on the other side of the door.

The argument had shifted from its original subject, which seemed to have been whether Grunwald would lend Hans money to pay gambling debts; now they were talking heatedly of Fleur Grunwald. Grunwald asked if Hans had had anything to do with Fleur's disappearance and Hans said he hoped he knew enough to stay out of domestic affairs. His laughter was rude and jeering, and struck Tristram to the heart. "I hope I am not so deprived as to be forced to content myself with another man's *well-used* property," he said.

Grunwald responded furiously. "If you have failed to force your attentions on Fleur, it is because you are too taken up by the manic crowd with which you run, and by the loathsome women in it. And by the fact of your own supreme, really quite extraordinary self-infatuation—"

"Look, Uncle, I am not *you*. I respect you as a businessman but I don't share your taste for women, as you must know. Enslaved, masochistic, failing, fainting, whining, whimpering, much-abused women. . . . Not for me: I prefer my women lusty and full-bodied and *healthy*."

"I won't hear of you insulting my wife! My poor Fleur!"

" 'Poor' Fleur indeed! What a joke! Who has made her 'poor,' but you, with your—"

"You know nothing of my marriage! How dare you! You know nothing, nothing of the happiness of the years Fleur and I have spent together—"

"Damn it, Uncle, I haven't come here to discuss *Fleur*; I don't even know that I knew she'd left you again,—what in God's name have I to do with that? My purpose in coming here is—"

"Is purely mercenary."

"—is *pure*, but not *mercenary*. I have certain debts which are gathering interest, and they must be paid, and *will* be paid, whether you—"

"Get out of my house! How dare you! Abusing my wife

to my very face, and begging for money! You do not deserve to live, a wretch like yourself—"

"And you, Uncle, deserve to live? Is that it? What a laugh! How do *you* dare—?"

"Get out of my house or I will call the police!"

Even so, the argument did not end; but continued, wide-ranging, bitter, and repetitious, for another fifteen or twenty minutes. By that time Tristram had prudently retreated to Grunwald's study, and was in the act of writing a note to his host,—*I hope you will excuse me but I thought it best to leave: perhaps we might speak at another time*—when Grunwald finally returned. He was trembling and white-faced but still indignant.

"My nephew means to destroy me with his spendthrift ways," he said bitterly, "but what am I to do?—he has youth on his side."

By now it was so late,—Tristram saw to his astonishment that it was nearly two o'clock in the morning: he had been in Grunwald's house almost seven hours—that Grunwald decided to curtail their visit after all. He was too exhausted and upset to continue, he said.

"But I hope we can meet again, soon, under more pleasant circumstances?" he said, as the men shook goodbye at the door. "For we have a good deal, I think, yet to discuss."

Tristram felt both relief and disappointment. But his handshake was firm, and his smile almost happy. "Yes, Mr. Grunwald," he said. "Soon."

6 The telephone was ringing. Close beside his head, ringing. And though he lay trapped in sleep heavy and dense as a block of ice Tristram could yet hear the woman's small gentle melodic voice, beseeching, pleading. *Why is the monster still living? Why, when you were within striking range? Why, if you claim to adore me as you do?*

With an enormous effort, as of one hurtling himself through a barrier, Tristram managed to wake; and fumbled to pick up the telephone receiver.

"Yes? Hello? Who is it? Hello?"

"Is this Tristram?—Tristram Heade?"

The voice was high-pitched, but male; an old man's voice, Tristram thought; and teasingly familiar. Guardedly Tristram said, "But who is this?" He had wakened groggily to a hotel room blazoned with light; his eyes watered, and his head began to throb, at first slowly, then with gathering violence. He had but the dimmest and most inchoate memory of the night before, at Otto Grunwald's house. . . .

"Is this my nephew Tristram Heade?"

"But who—who is speaking?"

"Tristram, is that you? It *is* you, isn't it?"

"But who are *you?*"

"Tristram?"

Even as the elderly man at the other end of the line identified himself as "Morris Heade,"—Tristram's great-uncle, whom he had been meaning to call for days—Tristram recognized his voice; and winced with guilt. Yet he said, calmly, "I'm afraid you have the wrong number, sir. There is no 'Tristram Heade' here."

"What? No Tristram there? But they told me at the desk—"

"There is no 'Tristram Heade' in this room."

"But you sound very like him. I would swear to it, you sound very like him." There was a brief silence. Tristram could hear the old man's labored breathing. "Tristram, *is* it you? I have been waiting for you to call, as you had promised. What on earth has happened?"

"I'm afraid, sir," Tristram said carefully, "you have the wrong number. My name is—well, it is not 'Tristram Heade.' "

"But this is the Hotel Moreau, isn't it? Room 608 of the Hotel Moreau, at Rittenhouse Square? They assured me at the desk that a party named 'Tristram Heade' of Richmond, Virginia, *was* registered for that room," the elderly man said, bewildered. "And you sound so very like my nephew! You were to have stayed at the Sussex, and you were to have telephoned me on your first evening, so that we could arrange for a quiet dinner here at the house. Why, you spoke with me only last week, from Richmond, and you sounded quite enthusiastic about the visit! What on earth has happened since then? Are you ill? Are you some sort of captive there?"

Tristram was perspiring badly, sitting bolt upright in his enormous bed, in his (or were they Markham's: the label boasted Harrod's) pajamas, amid a myopic daze of light. Where were his glasses? Why were they not on the bedside table, within easy reach? He had had too much to drink the night before and his head was beginning seriously to ache. Poor Uncle Morris! Tristram had not seen the old man in several years, and had always been very fond of him, and could not understand why, now, he was so desperate to elude him; but desperate he was. He might have thought, in the confusion of first waking, that the old man's appropriation of the telephone line prevented Fleur Grunwald from reaching him. . . .

Uncle Morris was saying, "Tristram? Are you there? Why won't you answer? Your cousin Beaumont was certain he'd seen you the other day in Rittenhouse Square, headed in the direction of a hotel called the Moreau, and as you were not at the Sussex, and they knew nothing of you—"

Tristram shut his eyes. "I'm afraid, sir, as I said—"

"My boy, what is it? Are you in trouble of some kind? Do you have a woman there with you, and are concerned that I might judge you harshly? I can't comprehend why, Tristram, you of all people, my favorite nephew, as you must know, would behave in so cruel and wanton a way toward me!"

"I know no one named 'Heade.' "

Tristram had no choice but to be rude: without another word he broke the connection. Perhaps someday he could explain the situation to his uncle, perhaps someday he and Fleur, happily married, would dine with the old man, and all would become, if not forgivable, at least exponible.

He then dialed the hotel switchboard, and instructed the operator that no further calls were to be put through for Tristram Heade. "And what of 'Angus Markham'?" the operater asked.

Tristram hesitated. " 'Angus Markham,' yes," he said. "But no one else."

And then he remembered, with a pang of guilt, that he had left his name and number with the lost-and-found office of the Philadelphia railway station . . . and should the "real" Angus Markham appear, hoping to claim his luggage, he would be unable to contact Tristram.

But, as things were so rapidly developing, Tristram was no longer eager to hear from Markham.

So far as he could determine, no more pieces of luggage had been delivered to his hotel room; no more of Markham's clothes were hanging in his closet. (Tristram had fallen into the habit of wearing both his own and Markham's clothes, without distinguishing between them, though he rather preferred Markham's to his own; except for the man's custom-made shoes, which were somewhat pointed in the toes, and more conspicuously stylish than Tristram liked.) Since his initial examination of the contents of the other man's valise, Tristram had not had time to examine them again, but a quick glance assured him that things were as they should be—the letters in their untidy packets, the scribbled-over racetrack forms, the real estate brochures. A melancholy odor as of several perfumes lifted to his nostrils. . . . It struck Tristram that, whatever the identity of the mysterious Markham, he was clearly a man to reckon with; not the sort of person who conveniently disappears, and clears the field for a rival.

"No. It is not like him. It would not be like *me*, in his place."

As if slantwise, the thought came to Tristram that Angus Markham might no longer be living. In which case he could never come forward to make his claim . . . of the valuables in the hotel room, or of Fleur Grunwald.

This thought both excited and worried him. If the man was dead, there must be a body; and where was the body? Tristram knew relatively little of criminal law, which had not been his field, but he did know that, without a body, without absolute proof of death, it was enormously difficult for police to investigate a crime; for the crime, if it lacked eyewitnesses, could only be conjectured. First-degree convictions in such murder cases are rare, even when circumstantial evidence is overwhelming. And missing adults in the United States are not ipso facto suspected of being victims any more than they are suspected of being criminals, for to be merely "missing" does not constitute a crime. The category means only that a human being has for some reason become invisible to certain others: not that he is invisible to all others, and not that he has met with what the law designates as "foul play."

Tristram could recall dimly, as if it had occurred not days but years ago, having glimpsed Angus Markham (or the man he presumed to be Markham) on the train . . . but he could recall virtually nothing about him. The category *man; adult male*; of Tristram's general build, and, perhaps, his age; conventionally well-dressed; presumably alone. Had he been murdered on the train, and his body thrown off? If only Tristram had looked directly into his face . . . if only their eyes had locked.

Tristram carried Markham's photograph in his wallet, with his own, for safekeeping, and now sought it out, and examined it thoughtfully. The handsome, arrogant face; the sweep of the blond hair; the level gaze; the firm set of the mouth and jaw. Perhaps Tristram imagined it, but the likeness had begun subtly to fade: the pale hair had grown paler, like a sort of nimbus, bleeding into the featureless background of the picture; the focus of the eyes was less distinctive than before. There was a cloudy smudge in the lower right-hand corner, like a ghostly thumbprint.

"Is he living, at this moment? Or is he dead?"

Suddenly the question struck Tristram as enormously, even urgently important. As important, in its own way, as the question of what he must do regarding Otto Grunwald. . . .

He could not go to the police, of course; he would have to hire a private investigator.

Already, even as the thought took shape, Tristram was at the telephone. He quickly looked up "detective agencies" in the Philadelphia directory, surprised to find so many listings, and chose one at random: Achilles Investigative Service ("Civil, Criminal & Domestic Investigations Our Specialty: All Phases Photographic Evidence—Professional Reports—Discreet Undercover Agents—Subpoena Service —Armed Bodyguards—Polygraph Service—Bonded & Licensed Agents—Affordable Fees—Free Initial Consultations—Call Anytime Day or Night"). So Tristram called, and made an appointment for later that morning, with a Mr. Handelman at the agency. He noted that, by a lucky coincidence, the office was in downtown Philadelphia, within walking distance of Rittenhouse Square.

Before setting out, Tristram made an attempt to speak with Fleur at the Delancy Street address; but could not get past a female he presumed to be her protectress, Otto Grunwald's cousin, who informed him that there was no one there except herself, and that the whereabouts of Fleur Grunwald were unknown to her. "I am in no way connected with Otto Grunwald," Tristram said carefully, "—I am Fleur's friend Angus Markham, who was there just yesterday. She must surely have told you about me? 'Angus Markham'?"

But the woman said only, "I'm sorry, Mr. Markham, Mrs. Grunwald is not here. I have no idea where she is."

"It's absurd to take that tone with me," Tristram said, rather hurt. "As I said, I was there just yesterday; I have your telephone number; I am—I am in love with Fleur, and have vowed to help her, as surely she has told you? When the horror has lifted the two of us will—"

"Mr. Markham, I'm afraid I will have to hang up now."

"Put her on the line! I insist you put her on the line! I have a message for her—put her on the line!"

There was a moment's hesitation; then the woman said, in a softer, yet still suspicious voice, "If Mrs. Grunwald were here—and if I could trust it that you *are* her friend, as you claim—what would that message be?"

Tristram said desperately, "That I love her."

When there was no response he added, "That I *adore* her."

When there was still no response he added, "That, tonight, it will be resolved. I vow that one way or another *it will be resolved.*"

But the line crackled dead in his ear.

"It is only that I lacked evidence," Tristram argued, "—as to whether the tattoos are genuine, or simulated. Indelible ink stitched into the very flesh or mere vegetable dye. How is a reasonable man to know? And how, not knowing, is one to act?"

He wondered too, in the sober light of day,—for it was uncommonly light, this midday in spring, with the consequence that his much-abused head ached—if one were justified in *blindly* and *extravagantly* believing the utterances of the unconscious; if, in short, he could believe Zoe's words, taking them as literal truth. For, apart from a single volume on the art of tattooing, amid Otto Grunwald's crowded collection of misogynist literature, there was nothing to link Grunwald with so barbaric a practice. And though Grunwald had spoken of a certain "purgative" operation for females —the specific name of which Tristram could not now recall, except to know that it was ugly-sounding—there was no reason to suspect that Grunwald himself had plans to mutilate his wife.

But: why had Tristram drunk so much! eaten so much! listened so unquestioningly to Otto Grunwald's arguments! And why had he so readily handed the glass eye over to the man?—when finding it was such an omen of Tristram Heade's own good luck?

"Perhaps I will get it back, tonight."

7 "Achilles Investigative Service" had its office on the sixth floor, rear, of an undistinguished office building on the busy corner of Eleventh and Broad streets, an unprepossessing address, like the tiny office itself, which rather disappointed Tristram in its dour, even dowdy, plainness. No romance in the colorless walls, the battered office furniture, the dust-shadowed slats of the venetian blinds; nor in the surprising fact that Mr. Handelman, for all his air of authority, energy, and enthusiasm, appeared to be alone in the office, with no receptionist or secretary. Indeed, almost as soon as Tristram stood hesitantly at the door, debating whether to rap on the opaque window glass, or walk in (ACHILLES INVESTIGATIVE SERVICE—WALK IN PLEASE! was painted on the glass), or quietly tiptoe away, a voice inside called out heartily, "Come in!"

He must have seen my shadow against the glass, Tristram thought.

"Bud" Handelman, as he introduced himself to Tristram, gave the impression of being preceded by his quick, tight, spasmlike smile; then came his quick, hard, spasmlike handshake. Small-bodied and boyishly sweet-faced, the sort of man invariably called wiry, Handelman was, so far as types of masculine personalities go, the very antithesis of Grunwald's nephew Hans; yet Tristram felt scarcely less uncomfortable in his presence. "Sit down! Sit down! Please sit down!" Handelman cried, even as Tristram was lowering himself into a springless leather chair, and facing the detective across an aluminum desk heaped with papers, dirtied Styrofoam coffee cups, and chocolate bar wrappers. Handelman appeared to be startlingly young, in his mid- or late twenties perhaps, but his manner was busily avuncular, gregarious, and peremptory. He wore a magenta-and-green checked sports coat, a pink-toned shirt open at the neck, and a pair of cuff links that resembled, at first glance, artificial tawny-gold eyes. His face was small, compact, and moon-shaped; his nose snubbed like a baby's; and though his glasses had thick lenses, suggesting extreme myopia, the lenses were tinted a fashionable violet-amber hue. Behind him on the wall, conspicuously placed, were several framed diplomas, a document stamped with the seal of the Commonwealth of Pennsylvania, certificates of merit, plaques, and photographs of Handelman in the company of other men, presumably satisfied clients, smiling into the camera. There were cheaply lacquered little signs too, above a hot-plate burner at Handelman's back, that read NO 'MYSTERY'—ONLY IGNORANCE!, and NO APPETITE TOO 'EVIL' TO BE CULTIVATED—OR TO BE DETECTED! Both remarks were attributed to Benjamin Franklin.

"You are the gentleman who just called? About a missing person? And who is the missing person, and when and where did you see him?" Handelman eagerly began, before Tristram could draw breath to speak. It was remarkable that, small as he was, no more than five feet three inches in height, and with that babyish face, the detective exuded the authority of a man of Tristram's size.

"—And did you bring a photograph?" Handelman added.

"Yes. Yes I did," Tristram said, feeling suddenly rather tongue-tied and vague. Why on earth had he come here? What force had drawn him here, to this peculiar little man's office, so far from home?

Handelman, as if reading Tristram's thoughts, urged him to speak frankly; and clearly; without inhibition; remembering that this was a free initial consultation, with no obligations, no strings attached. "Trust that we are entirely alone in this office, and all that you say will be kept *strictly confidential,*" he murmured, lowering his voice.

Tristram stared at the eager little man, who smiled at him with such hope, and gave off a faint air of staleness as of hope exuded on other occasions, and insufficiently washed away; wondering why had Angus Markham not guided him to a better detective, when the purpose of the transaction was after all to locate *him* . . . ?

Eventually, after a number of interruptions, including the distraction of a telephone that rang at Handelman's elbow, and was, flatteringly, not answered, Tristram managed to explain the situation, and his request, to Handelman, to the discreet degree to which he cared to explain it. (He said not a word of Fleur Grunwald of course. Nor of Otto Grunwald.) Yes there was a missing person, and his name was "Angus Markham"; and, yes, Tristram had brought along his photograph; but Tristram knew virtually nothing about the man other than his name, and his general appearance— "He resembles me, I've been told"—and the fact that he seemed to be involved in real estate transactions in Florida, and frequented racetracks, and was something of a ladies' man. Tristram thoughtfully provided Handelman with as much information as he knew of the train on which both he and Markham had been traveling, and ended with a rather vague and cursory summary of how, since that day, he, Tristram Heade, had been "mysteriously mistaken" for Angus Markham.

Nodding and murmuring enthusiastically, as if to encourage Tristram's recitation, as one might encourage a mildly retarded child, Handelman took lavish notes nonstop; covering sheets of paper in a large, wild scrawl. It troubled Tristram's sense of economy that only three or four lines of this scrawl could be accommodated on a single sheet of paper: surely this boded ill for the detective's expense account, for which the client had naturally to pay?

Tristram ended by saying carefully, "I want only to know

what has happened to Markham; I want to know his whereabouts, his address, telephone number, that sort of thing;
maybe a few photographs of him, if you can manage."
(Handelman nodded with a happy sort of impatience: of
course he could manage.) "I don't want to get in touch
with him, necessarily; and I *don't* want him to know that
anyone is—"

"Assuredly not, sir!" Handelman said, with an intake of
breath, as if Tristram had said something both foolish and
insulting.

"I want, as I said, only to know. My hope is to clear up
the mystery once and for all, simply to *know*—"

Handelman continued to take notes. " 'Simply to
know,'—'simply to *know*'—As if," he said, with a sudden
wink at Tristram, his eye magnified by the thick lens like a
fish that has swum up close against the glass wall of an
aquarium, "—*knowing were not everything.*"

Tristram could not quite comprehend the wink, but allowed it to pass. He remembered something he had meant
to ask earlier. "About your fee, Mr. Handelman—?"

"Ah yes my fee! My retainer, and my—fee!" Handelman
said, in a suddenly airy voice. His childlike eyes darted about
Tristram's person, as much of Tristram as he could see, both
men being seated; Tristram supposed the detective was as-
sessing the worth of the sharkskin suit he wore, the attractive
silk shirt, the bright Liberty print tie. Without intending it,
Tristram had dressed entirely in Markham's clothes today;
and had brought along, for some reason, the ebony walking
cane. . . . He will mistake me for a well-to-do man and demand an exorbitant fee, Tristram thought; and then remembered that he *was* a well-to-do man. (Since his parents'
death Tristram had lived frugally, with no real expenses except his antiquarian collection, and had managed, over the
years, to save a fair amount of money out of the interest
from his inheritance. But he understood that that way of
life in Richmond—monastic, celibate, "repressed"—was
now a thing of the past.)

Handelman did indeed suggest a fee that seemed to Tris-

tram rather steep, like a poker player bluffing a poor hand
(for Tristram understood that the detective badly wanted
the case), but the prospect of seeking out another agency
at this point was disagreeable. And Tristram had little time,
after all: there was the business with Grunwald tonight,
which might end in Grunwald's death . . . if Tristram's courage did not fail him. So Tristram agreed, and took out his
checkbook to make out the first check.

"I don't think you will be disappointed, Mr. Heade!"
Handelman said, licking his lips.

Handelman then picked up the photograph of Markham, which Tristram had laid on his desk, and proceeded
to examine it with care. He was so near-sighted he had to
bring it within an inch or two of his face. His smile froze;
then faded. Something about Markham's likeness so struck
him he did not even notice the check Tristram was holding
out to him. "Is something wrong? Do you know the man?"
Tristram asked. "Or isn't the photograph clear enough? It
seems to have faded a bit, since . . ."

Handelman, his childlike features now tightened in suspicion, or in dread, was looking from the photograph to
Tristram, comparing the two. Tristram felt a pang of uneas-
iness. Does he think I am that man? Does he think this is
some sort of trick? he wondered. Or does he know Angus
Markham, and fear him?

"What is it, Mr. Handelman?" Tristram asked, suddenly
desperate. "Don't you want to take the case after all?"

But still, so very oddly, Handelman did not speak! In the
awkward silence Tristram became aware of traffic noises lifting from the street, and of a woman's high-heeled shoes
clattering, and fading, in the corridor outside Handelman's
door, and, in the wall close beside him, a small, furious,
scratching sound, as of a trapped animal. . . . Handelman
carefully laid down the photograph of Markham, and
picked up Tristram's check, and stared at it, licking his lips.
An expression of greed overlaid with regret—or was it regret overlaid with greed—showed in his face. For a long
terrible moment Tristram was sure that Handelman was go-

ing to rip the check in two. "What *is* it?" Tristram asked. "Do you want more money?"

Handelman shook his head almost irritably, as if the very question were an insult. "Not at all," he said, swallowing hard, "—a deal is a deal." In that instant it was decided: he flashed his quick bright brave smile, and rose from his chair to shake Tristram's hand. "You are my client, Mr. Heade, in this 'Markham' business, and I am your man. *Invincible and unbribable*—the motto of Achilles!"

Tristram, taller than the detective by a head, and heavier by one hundred pounds, could not help but wince at the ferocity of the little man's handshake.

Minutes later Tristram was waiting for the elevator, lost in thought—though what he was thinking of he could not have said, his brain so bedazzled—when a high-pitched voice rang out along the corridor, badly startling him. It was Handelman, who came limping (limping!) after him, brandishing Markham's shiny black cane like a child's sword.

The detective had entirely regained his exuberance. "You don't want to forget *this*, Mr. Heade!" he cried, his left eye screwed up in a wink.

IV

1

And wilderness is Paradise enough.

These words of Omar Khayyám's rang in Tristram's head as he climbed over the wrought iron fence at the rear of the Grunwald estate, and made his way through the shadows to the house itself, his heart beating pleasantly fast and his senses keenly aroused. It was an intermittently moonlit night; a night of winds; high-scudding clouds; breathlessness. Tristram could not have said if it were cunning, or instinct, or an admixture of both, that led him in the patchy dark to the window opening into Otto Grunwald's study; *his* window; the window he had rendered safe for his entry.

Hours before, at dusk, Tristram had taken a cab to Fairmount Park; to the northernmost corner of the park, a discreet distance from Burlingham Boulevard. He was dressed quite conventionally, in a suit and a tie, but carried a duffel bag containing the costume into which, in one of the park's public restrooms, he quickly changed: dark gray gabardine trousers, black turtleneck jersey shirt, black tennis shoes, black beret. All these items, with the exception of the beret, Tristram had discovered in Markham's largest suitcase. (The beret, purchased in a pricey gentlemen's shop in the Hotel Meridian,—*not* in the Moreau, where the purchase might be traced—was Tristram's own idea, or so he believed, since his hair had grown rather long, and was likely to call attention to itself in the dark.) He had a length of cord; a flashlight; a pair of kidskin gloves that fitted his hands nearly as tightly as a surgeon's rubber gloves; and, of course, Markham's finely honed dagger.

(Perhaps it was Tristram's imagination, but the dagger seemed sharper, and even a little larger, than previously. The mere weight of it in his hand, its physicality, its *presence,* helped to placate his fears, for he reasoned that a weapon that had performed well for its owner in the past could not fail to perform well for its owner again.)

Tristram had little difficulty in forcing the window to Grunwald's study, and scarcely more difficulty climbing through, though the maneuver was new to him, and would have been dauntingly tricky had he stopped and calculated how to do it instead of trusting to instinct. He might have thought himself too large and ungainly to fit through the rather narrow space; he would surely have bungled the upward-heaving of his body, which seemed to defy gravity, its weight concentrated for several astonishing seconds merely on his forearms, which rested on the windowsill. But his arm and shoulder muscles, and even the muscular tissue of his hands, were more powerful than he might have thought; and, where only a few days ago, in Richmond, he would have been seriously winded from such exertion, he now felt rather invigorated.

"So this is what I have been cheated of, for most of my life!"

And now, as if in a dream, he found himself in Otto Grunwald's study; in the man's very house. *And no one knew he was here.*

He switched on the flashlight, and shone a quick darting penetrating light into the corners of Grunwald's study, illuminating in turn the fireplace and its marble mantel . . . shelves of books . . . the several glass-fronted cabinets . . . the twin skeletons wired to their poles . . . the desk, chairs, lamps, carpet . . . the closed door that led to the corridor. (Though he knew they were there, Tristram was momentarily startled by the sight of "Adam" and "Eve," and nearly dropped his flashlight. How horrific, those eyeless grinning faces!—if, in the strictest sense, skeletons have faces.)

As quickly as he could manage, yet not in careless haste, Tristram searched the drawers of Grunwald's desk, finding, for the most part, little of interest; a good many financial records, and letters pertaining to business, philanthropy, and charity; collectors' brochures and printouts, of the kind Tristram kept in his own desk, in Richmond; and, in one drawer, a folder stuffed with newspaper and magazine clippings dating back to the early 1960s—features on black-tie benefit dinners in Philadelphia, cocktail receptions, brunches, and the like. Photographed sometimes with other couples, sometimes by themselves, were "Mr. and Mrs. Otto Grunwald": beautiful Fleur, looking very young, standing beside her husband with the faintest of posed smiles. . . . The sight of her pierced Tristram to the heart. How he loved her! Adored her! *Mr. and Mrs. Otto Grunwald at the opening night of "La Traviata," a benefit performance for the American Association for the Advancement of Mental Health . . . Mr. and Mrs. Otto Grunwald at the opening of the Van Gogh exhibit, at the Philadelphia Museum of the Arts.* . . . A little further down, however, he discovered, to his disgust, that "Mrs. Otto Grunwald" did not necessarily mean Fleur Grunwald; a wife preceded her, and a wife preceded that wife, both of them young-looking, and beautifully dressed, but not, he thought, so beautiful as Fleur.

Poor things! he thought, stung with pity. You had no "Angus Markham" to save you.

Next, thinking to find a safe, Tristram removed a painting from the wall directly behind Grunwald's desk, discovering instead a curious little lever which, after a moment's hesitation, he turned; and to his surprise—unless perhaps it was *not* to his surprise—the wall panel slid noiselessly open, and another room was revealed. "This is it," Tristram said, with a sharp intake of breath. " 'Master's cave.' "

It was supremely quiet. Only the mantel clock's quiet ticking and Tristram's own warm, rhythmic breathing sounded in his ears.

The secret room was windowless, unlike the other, to which it seemed a sort of twin—having approximately the same dimensions as the other, and furnished and decorated in the same style. But how different this room was!—how frightful, and repulsive, to Tristram's eye!

The walls were almost completely covered with obscene works of art: paintings, drawings, etchings, photographs; all of them featuring women, naked or scantily clad women, in various poses of wantonness, shamelessness, seductiveness, humiliation, pain, ecstasy, bondage. So much flesh, and so lewdly exposed! In a corner of the room, discreetly hidden by a richly brocaded Japanese silk screen, was a leather table very like a doctor's examination table, equipped with stirrups, straps, and buckles; and a cabinet of what appeared to be tattooing equipment. "So Zoe spoke the truth!" Tristram said aloud, directing his light, with a fascinated sort of dread, on shelves of sinister glittering needles, bottles of brightly colored dyes, and various clinical and pharmaceutical items. A sickish odor of chloroform overlaid with an odor of tobacco smoke pressed against his nostrils.

"He is a beast after all."

And yet the flashlight, trembling in Tristram's hand, illuminated still more horrors: a riding crop stained with blood . . . several pairs of handcuffs . . . a length of rope . . . leg-irons . . . chains of various sizes . . . a rack of wickedly gleaming scalpels, syringes, knives. There was a clear plastic container of swabs of cotton batting, into which used swabs had been carelessly tossed, their bloodstains faded to brown like autumn leaves. There was a shelf of books with such titles as *The Ancient Art of Tattooing, 1001 Easy Designs for the Amateur Tattooist, "Forbidden" Tattoos of the Southsea Islands.* Tristram examined the last-named, which opened readily to a lavish peacock-tail design, all brilliant blues, greens, and purples, a tapestry of tiny eyes lewdly tattooed on a woman's body. The woman was kneeling, facing away from the camera, head bowed so dramatically low it seemed at first glance she might be headless.

"Beast. *Bastard.*"

The flashlight's beam lifted to the walls, to expose in sequence a framed reproduction of Peter Paul Rubens's

"Angelica and the Monk" . . . a Japanese woodcut of naked females busily engaged in lesbian orgies . . . a luridly colored photograph of a whipped black girl hanging by her bound wrists from a beam, bleeding from dozens of long snaky red-glistening wounds . . . drawings and paintings of wicked nymphs, coy madonnas, slyly beckoning odalisques, aloofly erotic "chimeras" . . . sphinxes, witches, Venuses, femmes fatales both fleshy and cadaverous, salacious and mock-chaste, gorgeous and repulsive . . . reproductions of nudes by Goya, Boucher, Toulouse-Lautrec, Aubrey Beardsley, Gustav Klimt, Egon Schiele, Picasso, Salvador Dalí. . . . Tristram's cheeks burned. He felt an adolescent's puritanical anger; and an adolescent's immediate sexual arousal.

And then he was thinking of Fleur; and of Zoe. How the woman had coiled her bare arms around his neck, and pressed her eager, heated body against his; how she had allowed him to bury his face in her neck, and kiss her lips; running his hands over her smooth naked body . . . her hips, her thighs, her breasts, her belly . . . the barbarous tattoos stitched in her very flesh, ineradicable. Ah, Tristram had been mad for her! Mad, crazed, frantic with desire!

Of course, Tristram thought, trying to calm his excitement, she was not to blame.

Not to blame for tempting him, tormenting him with lust.

No reasonable man could blame Otto Grunwald's wife for bizarre behavior; for unnatural behavior of any kind. Victimized as hardly more than a child by the brute's sick appetites, systematically terrorized, disfigured, humiliated, debased. . . . But, ah, that teasing maddening singsong!— Zoe's lascivious *knowingness* sounding in the bell-like purity of Fleur's *innocence*.

Be still says He and you will not be hurt.

Hideous. Filthy. Unspeakable.

And yet . . .

Tristram recalled uneasily that Zoe had hinted (or had she more than hinted) that Fleur was an accomplice of a kind in these perverted practices; and had not Grunwald hinted, or charged, more or less the identical thing? Grunwald had accused Fleur too of spreading slanderous tales about him in Philadelphia, in the hope of getting a larger divorce settlement than the law would probably have granted; and of having a lover. *A man met at the racetrack at Saratoga.*

"But I am that man," Tristram said aloud. "Am I not that man?"

He was staring at the reflection of a pale, angry-looking stranger in a mirror tilted above the examination table; a man who resembled him, but wore a black beret that covered most of his longish blond hair, was perspiring visibly, and had the jaws of a predator.

The stranger grinned at him. He had found the evidence, hadn't he! The woman had spoken the truth! No further proof was required: the next step was to climb the stairs to the second floor, and seek out Otto Grunwald in his bed, and murder him as he slept. Or should the monster be awakened first, and then murdered? *Taking yourself by surprise you take your quarry by surprise as well.*

Except . . .

And yet . . .

Suppose it were true that Fleur Grunwald, in her innocence, had acquiesced to her husband's wishes? That, having married a much older and very wealthy man, presumably not for love (Tristram winced at the thought), the young woman had . . . if not exactly brought her fate upon herself, at least invited it? Collaborated in it? In all fairness it must be said that Fleur's intensely feminine passivity might well have provoked Grunwald's "masculine" sadism. In which case, was Grunwald guilty? or, in his own way, innocent? Guilty of unspeakable, vile behavior; yet innocent too . . . in a way?

Or might both be guilty, and both innocent?

Tristram recalled, however, from law school, that certain crimes remain crimes even if the victim allegedly consents.

Thus, to aid and abet a suicide is to violate the statute against manslaughter; to kill someone who asks to be killed is to commit murder nonetheless.

Tristram dared not meet his own impatient stare in the mirror. "If only I knew. If only I . . . could be certain."

So minutes passed, in indecision. The more Tristram pondered the ambiguity of the situation, the subtleties and contradictions of the moral issues involved, the more distracted he became, until he was oblivious of his surroundings, and of the danger of his position. He was standing with his back to the door, his eyes half shut; more anxious, more apprehensive, than he had been while breaking into Grunwald's house. Like a man straddling a wall who has forgotten in which direction he is heading he truly did not know what to do next. There was Fleur, whom he hoped to marry; but there was also Zoe, whom, perhaps, he rather dreaded. And there was Otto Grunwald, admittedly a monster, and undeserving of life, yet, if one were to be fair-minded, perhaps he too was a "victim" . . . a "victim of his own desires" as the popular phraseology would have it.

And hadn't Grunwald been extremely friendly to Tristram; like an uncle, or an older brother? Like a father? *Call me Otto, please call me Otto, why cannot you bring yourself to call me Otto?*

Poor Tristram was overcome by these thoughts when, with no more warning than a quick scuttling sound behind him, he was struck a blow to the back of the head with what felt like a hammer, and staggered, and reeled, and—and did not quite lose consciousness; but managed to push off his assailant who was (or so it appeared: in the struggle the flashlight had gone flying) Otto Grunwald himself.

There followed then one of those brief yet prolonged episodes of a kind that determine a life; desperate, even frenzied, yet in a dreamlike way coolly performed. There was no light except the faintest, gauziest light, a mere nimbus of light, since Tristram's flashlight had rolled to a far corner of the room, and cast its most concentrated beam merely against a wall; and the struggle, for all its violence, took place without words.

Though the larger of the two men, and, with his newly hardened muscles, certainly the stronger, Tristram was so stunned by the blow to his head that he could not wrestle his opponent away from him, in order to strike him, or to pull Markham's dagger out of his pocket. Grunwald (or the man Tristram presumed to be Grunwald) had, in the struggle, dropped his weapon, but was so ferocious in his attack, so intent upon beating Tristram into unconsciousness, it seemed initially that he might win . . . and would then (of this, Tristram had no doubt) have the privilege of finishing off his opponent.

(I have violated the man's inner sanctum, Tristram thought. He would rather die, and would far rather commit murder, than have it be known.)

Groping about behind him, Grunwald snatched up the riding crop, and struck Tristram a stinging blow to the side of the head; and Tristram, now desperate, seized Grunwald about the hips, and threw him backward against the examination table. Grunwald groaned in pain and surprise: one of the stirrups must have caught him in the small of the back. But in an instant he was on Tristram again . . . embracing him and wrestling him to the floor . . . where, rolling over and over, striking out wildly with their fists and elbows, pummeling, kicking, gouging, choking, ferocious but uncoordinated as children, the men struggled together for what seemed like a very long time but could not have been more than two or three minutes. Tristram had by now forgotten the dagger in his pocket; had forgotten his sacred mission; had forgotten who he was, and what force had brought him to this strange place where he was fighting to the death with a man whose face he could not see clearly, a man who seemed intent upon killing him. How was it possible? *Was* it possible? —With a crash, the Japanese screen was knocked over, and a metal stand holding trays of tattooing equipment went skidding into a wall, and the glass front of a cabinet shattered loudly—all of which, Tristram thought, in a normal household, would have drawn the servants. But Grunwald's staff must have been conditioned to ignore, perhaps not even to hear, strange noises rising from Master's cave. . . .

By degrees Tristram's superior strength and weight took their toll. Grunwald began to tire, breathing so laboriously, giving off such desperate heat, Tristram worried he might have a heart attack or a stroke: which would, in this context, constitute murder if he were to die. Tristram panted, "Let me go! And I promise not to hurt you!" But the elder man lashed out savagely at him, and would have closed his fingers around Tristram's neck had not Tristram caught his wrists, and shoved him backward. His head struck something on the wall, and glass flew out into Tristram's face, momentarily blinding him. In the confusion of the moment Tristram thought, It is the madman's glass eye, and now he will be stopped.

The fight did in fact end shortly, with Grunwald too exhausted to continue, slumped on the floor, and Tristram able at last to make his retreat. With no thought for his purpose in having come here he snatched up the flashlight, and ran blindly away: running, it seemed, for his very life.

2 Running for his very life: along deserted Burlingham Boulevard, where the enormous sepulchral homes of Grunwald's neighbors were hidden in darkness . . . into the moon-splotched shadows of Fairmount Park, which, by night, had acquired a sinister yet dreamlike atmosphere, silent except for the cry of a screech owl in the distance . . . in a state of mind, or of nerves, unlike any he had experienced previously in his life. How close he had come to killing another human being! And yet, how sick with disgust he would be, shortly, how revolted at his own cowardice, when the reality of what he had done—what he had failed to do—sank in. I have allowed the monster to live, he thought. Fleur will never marry me now: will never so much as look at me again.

So he ran, and walked, and ran; hearing the sound of footsteps somewhere behind him; which, when he listened closely, seemed abruptly to fade. Had Grunwald sent someone after him? Was Grunwald himself in pursuit? Tristram's heart lurched against his ribs. His body was covered with perspiration.

It had been his intention originally to change his clothes again; to return to the Hotel Moreau by taxi, as he had left it, in the suit in which he had departed, having disposed of his other clothes, as well as the duffel bag, the rope, the flashlight, the "murder weapon." He had secreted the duffel bag behind some bushes in the park but could not now recall its location, no more than he could recall how he had expected to find a taxi in this part of the city, at this time of night. . . .

He had even lost the beret. He prayed he had not lost it in Grunwald's house.

Were there patrolmen on duty in the park? Was he being observed? Though officially closed at sunset, this enormous park was surely a place in which many might hide . . . derelicts, criminals . . . madmen. Its utter stillness reminded him of the Black Forest, in which he had hiked years ago as a young man touring Germany. Or had it been Angus Markham who had hiked in the Black Forest?

The footsteps behind him were more pronounced. Someone was certainly following him. A policeman would have shone a light on him and commanded him to stop, but this pursuer followed in absolute silence, as wordless as Grunwald had been in his savage attack.

This time, Tristram thought grimly, it will be to the death.

Instinct guided him into a pedestrian tunnel leading beneath a park road; the sort of place, debris-littered, puddled, smelling of decayed leaves and human urine, in which vagrants sometimes take refuge. Tristram's fastidious nostrils contracted against the stench. The tunnel was long . . . longer than seemed possible . . . a horror of echoing footsteps and the sound, or sounds, of trickling water. In the distance Tristram could hear the eerie, chilling, yet melodic cry of the screech owl; and was reminded, with a pang of hurt, of home; of the home lost to him now; wrenched from him as forcibly and as cruelly as valuables are wrenched from a mugging victim. This too he blamed on Otto Grunwald.

Shrewdly, Tristram pressed himself against the side of the tunnel; and waited. The far end of the tunnel was so distant, its aperture so faintly illuminated by moonlight, his pursuer would be unable to see him silhouetted against it. The man had boldly entered the tunnel; was making his way forward gropingly; his breath coming in quick snorting pants. It was

Grunwald of course for who else could it be? He wants my heart, Tristram thought. Nothing less will satisfy him.

This time Tristram was prepared: Markham's dagger in hand, and his fingers closed firmly about it. And when his pursuer passed close beside him Tristram leapt upon him with the fury of an unleashed predatory beast; and, giving the astonished man no time to defend himself, let alone attack, struck him numberless blows with the knife: to the chest, to the throat, to the arms, shoulders, belly, loins. He paid no heed to the man's terrified cries and his pleas for mercy—"No! No! I beg of you! Let me live!" Nor did he pay much heed to the warm blood that spurted forth, as if by cruel magic, from each stabbing blow of the dagger.

Then the man lay silent and unmoving at Tristram's feet, in a trickle of fetid water. "There. That's done," Tristram said, with satisfaction.

He wiped the dagger's blade on some leaves close by; then walked off a few feet, and paused, and listened, his head cocked to one side, before leaving the tunnel's shelter. But no: there was no further sound.

Not even the screech owl.

3 And in the morning Tristram received one of the great shocks of his life.

The *Philadelphia Inquirer*, delivered to his hotel room, was ablaze with headlines announcing the death of "Otto S. Grunwald, Philadelphia businessman and philanthropist": but the accompanying photograph, of a smiling, crinkle-eyed gentleman, bore only a glancing resemblance to the man Tristram had met; and the accompanying story had it that Grunwald had been found dead in his study, *in his home on Burlingham Boulevard,* the probable victim of a would-be burglar or burglars. "But he died in the park, in the tunnel," Tristram said, stunned. "If he died at all he did not die *there.*" With trembling fingers Tristram held the newspaper aloft, close to his face, and read and reread all that pertained to Grunwald. There was even a photograph of Fleur on an inside page, taken the previous autumn at a benefit dinner for the American Red Cross. Posed in a high-necked long-sleeved dress with her arm formally linked through that of the tuxedo-clad Grunwald, lovely Fleur stared at the camera so strangely, smiled so small, tight, secret a smile, Tristram almost did not recognize her.

"If he died at all . . . he did not die *there.*"

And, on page forty-nine, there was a two-line headline in very small type, to the effect that a homeless man by the name of Poins—"a familiar habitant of Fairmount Park, known to locals for his faithful proselytizing of a 'prophet' by the name of Bruno Love"—had been found in a pedestrian tunnel in the park by an early-morning jogger. The three-inch article noted that Poins had once been a well-respected mathematician and had taught for twenty-five years at the University of Pennsylvania; that he had lived in the area of the park for the past decade, or more; that "no known motive" was given for the killing, in which the victim "suffered more than thirty stab wounds" over much of his body. There was no accompanying photograph.

"Poins! The madman! *Him!* —Did I kill *him?*"

Tristram let the newspaper fall to the floor, and passed a hand over his eyes. He could not understand it. He had fled like a coward from Otto Grunwald's home, having *not* killed him there; yet the man was dead, had been found by servants in a room tactfully described as "an extension of his library," the victim, like poor Poins, of "multiple stab wounds."

Had he killed Grunwald after all, without intending it? without remembering it? Or had someone else killed Grunwald? —But the coincidence would be too great: another intruder, another break-in, at the very same hour.

No. It was too much of a coincidence.

And he *had* killed Poins, obviously. He distinctly remembered crouching in the tunnel, awaiting his pursuer, raising the dagger high, and higher still. . . . "Did I really do such a thing? *I?* Tristram Heade?" A violent shudder ran through his body. *"But why did I do it?"*

The telephone was ringing; had perhaps been ringing for some time; half consciously Tristram reached out to pick up the receiver, and heard a woman's voice speaking his name.

That is, "Angus! Angus!"

It was Fleur Grunwald, sobbing, it seemed, with grief— or was it joy—her words coming so incoherently at first, Tristram could scarcely understand what she said. Yet the substance of it was, so far as he could assess, that she was "eternally grateful" to him and would "eternally adore" him—and would come by taxi to his hotel at once.

Tristram had been standing rigid, if not paralyzed; in his, or Markham's, dressing gown; his head ringing, and his eyeballs aching as if he had stared too long into a bright beam of light. He had heaved himself out of bed with enormous effort some forty-five minutes before, and had not taken time to shower, or even to shave; his fingers were sticky with a reddish-brown substance (which could only, he supposed, in these circumstances, be blood), and he felt, overall, as queasy, as uncertain, as demoralized, as depressed, as he had ever felt in his life; like a seasoned gambler—the analogy flew into Tristram's head from he knew not where—who has won the first race at the track, and has taken his winnings and bet again; and won; and taken those winnings and bet again; and won yet again; and has taken *those* winnings (by this time a deliriously large sum), and has dared to bet again . . . in defiance even of his premonition that Luck, that expendable quantity, has expended itself quite enough already on his behalf. And here was Fleur Grunwald's call, and here, so intimate in his ear, her voice; and the promise that she was coming to him at once; the promise, or its implication, that she was at last *his.*

"That is some consolation, at least," Tristram heard himself say, thoughtfully.

He had not returned to the Hotel Moreau, and to the safety of his suite, until nearly dawn. And then afoot; and appearing, he had no doubt, much the worse for wear—his trousers torn, muddied, and stained with dried blood; his hands stained too; his hair dishevelled; his gait swaying and uncertain as a derelict's. The uniformed doorman, of whom, with his generous tipping, he had made a loyal friend, did not do much more than blink in sympathetic surprise at the apparition he presented; then proceeded to brush him off, to the extent to which he could, with his gloved hands. There were fragments of dried leaves in Tristram's clothing and hair; even, in his hair, as he would discover up in his room, that confettilike substance, transparent, but colored, found in children's Easter baskets. When he reached into his pocket to give the doorman a tip his fingers closed upon a hard, stonelike object, which he instinctively let go: it would be Otto Grunwald's artificial eye.

And so, as he discovered in the elevator, it was.

"An eye for an eye," he whispered.

Though in fact he was rather shaken, for he had not seriously believed at the time that the artificial eye had popped out of Grunwald's head when Tristram had slammed him against the wall; the thought had been sheerly notional, a panicked whim, the consequence of the extreme emotional duress in which he had been at the time. . . . Yet here was the eye, tremulously resting in the palm of Tristram's hand! His defeated enemy's left eye, made not of old-fashioned glass but of some extraordinarily lightweight synthetic substance, a kind of plastic, he supposed. The "white" of the eye was a yellowish-ivory shade, which ingeniously matched the slightly sullied look of the human eye; the iris was a faded brown, flecked with bits of hazel like mica. *The precise mate of the dead man's living eye.* But what am I meant to do with it? Tristram wondered, shuddering. I can't keep it, but it would be too cruel to . . . dispose of it. He seemed to sense that even Angus Markham, that most practicable and least sentimental of men, would draw the line at "disposing" of the eye.

Up in his room, Tristram breathed a deep sigh of relief. He had journeyed long and far in order to exact his revenge; and had not, in the end,—whether out of weakness, or oversensitivity—exacted that revenge except (for so he reasoned, at this time) in self-defense. So he had rescued poor Fleur from her marriage, but not at the cost (for so he reasoned, at this time) of a merely wanton, gratuitous act. "You gave me no choice," Tristram said, placing the eye carefully in the ashtray atop his bureau, where the other artificial eye had been.

Tristram then pulled off his filthy clothes, and fell almost insensible into his bed; and slept the kind of deep, ponderous, soul-restoring sleep with which he had come to associate that particular bed.

(In one of his dreams, which he was not to recall until after Fleur's arrival and departure that morning, Tristram saw himself approach his mirrored reflection with his right hand extended . . . and saw the reflection extend its right hand to him . . . so that the two men, or, rather, Tristram and his mirror-self, shook hands. "I am so happy," Tristram whispered, "—why has no one ever told me, in all of my previous life, of such happiness?" But the mirror-self was not, he saw upon closer inspection, Tristram Heade; it was another man, a stranger—a just perceptibly older, thicker-bodied, ruddier-faced, slightly ravaged Angus Markham. Markham pointed to his left eye, saying silently, *It is the fact that the iris is surrounded by white that accounts for its look of terror;* then, before Tristram could respond, *You should not have set a mercenary spy on my trail* ran through Tristram's thoughts in the same quicksilver fashion, like ripples running silently through water. And then the dream rapidly dissolved, and Tristram was left alone again, his heart pierced by a profound melancholy.)

"I can't believe it. *I am a free woman at last.*"

Fleur did not throw herself into Tristram's arms, as he had hoped she might; but, visibly trembling, her lovely eyes welling with tears, she clasped his hand in both her black-gloved hands, and drew so close to him he halfway thought, inhaling her fragrance, that she might lean forward on her toes and kiss him in childlike gratitude. Her skin was pale and luminous, the cheeks lightly flushed as if with fever; the irises of her eyes were so dilated as to appear nearly black. A strand of golden-brown hair fell loosely across her forehead and tempted Tristram to smooth it back into place. . . . How the sight of her rocked him, to his very soul! In her excited state Fleur was even more beautiful than he recalled. And though she wore black, layers of black, a smart black woolen jacket atop a pleated black silk blouse, a black skirt that fell nearly to her ankles, black textured stockings and shining black patent-leather shoes,—though the woman's body was covered, cloaked, from ankle to neck, and from neck to wrist—Tristram could well imagine, with a swoon of desire, what lay beneath. Here stands my fate before me, he thought.

Shedding the blood of any number of men was worth it, for *this.*

But Tristram dared not embrace Fleur quite yet, dared not display his passion too roughly. (And it was passion, indeed: sudden, fierce, *manly.*) His handclasp made her wince, the very expression in his face seemed to intimidate her. She could only stay with him a few minutes this morning, she said; her life—her "newly widowed life"—would be disagreeably public for some time. For overnight, in the space of an hour, she had become a wealthy woman.

"It was one of the terms of our . . . agreement," Fleur said softly, gazing up at Tristram with wide dilated eyes. Her lips drew back repeatedly from her small even white teeth in a twitching smile. "Otto agreed to leave me most of his fortune, if I would consent to marry him; not a penny, he said, to his relatives, who, he claimed, were always spying on him, and talking of him behind his back, and waiting for him to die. His despicable nephew Hans was the most blatant! Of course there will be sizable sums, amounting to millions, given away to charity,—to those charities whose organizers succeeded in flattering Otto the most—but not a penny, not a penny," she cried, laughing up at Tristram, "—to the Grunwalds. To the very people who have for so many years been snubbing *me*!"

Tristram said, "It is no more than you deserve."

"It is no more than I have *earned,*" Fleur said fiercely. "Of course Otto was in the process of altering his will, to eliminate me entirely, since I fled him and vowed, this time, never to return; of course he was outraged, wounded in his pride, and would have done anything within his power to defeat me, but he could not have foreseen *you.* That *you* would reappear again in my life, and transform it completely. I know, I know, Angus," she said quickly, laying a hand on Tristram's arm in reassurance, "—that it isn't anything more than coincidence, your arrival here in Philadelphia and my desperate appeal to you,—to all that is decent, kindly, noble, courageous, generous, and manly in you!— and the fact of, of what happened last night, to poor Otto. Set upon as he was by a thief, or thieves, and stabbed to death *in the very 'cave' of his crimes.* It isn't anything other than coincidence, and we will speak of it no further. We will never speak of it, dear Angus! Never!" And in an impulsive childlike gesture she lay her gloved forefinger against her lips.

Tristram was suffused with pleasure; and gratitude at *her* gratitude; but said, "One thing does worry me, dear, a bit— You said that the Grunwalds have been cut out of your husband's will? Including that rather surly young nephew—"

Fleur shuddered and looked away. "Hans. As much a beast as his uncle. I'm sorry that you had to encounter him."

"Do you think,"—Tristram paused delicately, "—he might cause trouble, over the will? Cause *us* trouble?"

With a visibly trembling hand Fleur shaded her eyes, and seemed unable to speak. Then she said, faintly, "Please don't force me to think of such possibilities now, Angus. Not now. Please don't spoil my joy in my relief, in my *release,* dear Angus, if you love me, now!"

"Of course I love you," Tristram said, utterly rapt. All thoughts of Hans fled from his brain; all thoughts of Otto Grunwald's fury, and the mystery of his death; all thoughts too of the luckless Poins, of whom this innocent young woman knew nothing. Tristram edged toward her, wanting very badly to take her in his arms. But did he dare? In her state of nerves? Did even Markham dare? "—I love you, darling Fleur, as you must know, since I have proved it. We will never speak of it again, of course,—but I have proved it. I want to marry you, and take you away from this city, and we can begin again, in another part of the world, as husband and wife, in whom everything will be renewed." Tristram paused and swallowed hard, seeing the look of sudden maidenly fright in Fleur's face. "As soon, I mean, as propriety allows."

Fleur continued to stare at the floor, or at the cruelly pointed toe of her patent-leather pump. It seemed to Tristram that she nodded . . . or did not quite nod.

"We *are* to be married, Fleur—aren't we?"

Again, the nod of her lovely head was near-imperceptible. Her cheeks appeared warm, and her eyes too brightly shining. She is as stricken with joy as I, Tristram thought, but does not know how to express it. The wavy strand of golden-brown hair had slipped further into her face, and Fleur brushed it away with a nervous gesture. "As soon as propriety allows," she whispered, blushing.

Tristram's hungry gaze took in the young woman's elegantly black-clad figure; dropped to her slender ankles, lifted slowly to her hips, her waist, her breasts. . . . With a pang of desire he recalled Zoe's wild embrace; her arms coiling around his neck; he could feel again the urgency of her warm panting breath. He knew that beneath the artful camouflage of her clothes Fleur Grunwald was astonishingly beautiful; as beautiful as any of the fleshy images on Otto Grunwald's secret walls; and that her beauty was not marred by the tapestry of wildly colored tattoos that covered it, but enhanced. And it seemed to provoke Tristram's desire the more, that he *knew*, and had *seen*; and that Fleur (if Zoe spoke the truth) knew nothing of his knowledge.

As if reading Tristram's thoughts, Fleur backed from him, her expression now confused, the spasmodic smile twitching at her lips. In a nearly inaudible voice she said, "I—I am not worthy. I think that you—if you—if things were— I think, Angus," she said, her voice lifting bravely, "—I think you would find me despoiled."

"Find you—?"

"Despoiled."

Fleur turned abruptly away, and hid her face in her hands. A shaft of pale sunshine, filtered through the gauzy inner curtain of the tall window, illuminated, as if in a rare work of art, the gold-glinting highlights of her hair, and the drops of moisture, like iridescent pearls, that fell from her eyes.

Tristram could bear it no longer. He went to embrace her, and pressed his lips against her mouth; and Fleur gave a little scream, high-pitched and piercing as a child's; and seemed almost to leap out of his arms. "No!" she cried. "Oh please!"

"Fleur, for God's sake!" Tristram said, rather more harshly than he wished.

His instinct was to seize the woman's wrist, to calm her; but she backed cowering away from him, arms lifted in feeble self-protection, and her widened eyes showing white around the iris. Tristram froze where he stood, staring at her.

Fleur said quickly, "I'm so sorry! Dear Angus! I—I can't seem to help myself—it must have something to do with *him*. Please believe me when I say that I love you; I love no one but you; I am eternally in your debt, for reasons of which we cannot speak. I want to marry you, I *will* marry you, but—"

"But you imagine yourself 'despoiled'!" Tristram said.

"—And so much has happened in so short a space of time," Fleur pleaded, "—surely you can sympathize with me? I had to flee Otto so quickly, and all the while I hid at Delancy Street I knew the madman would do virtually anything to get me back, and revenge himself upon me." She stared at Tristram with tear-filled eyes, biting her lower lip like a repentant child. "But please believe me—I do love you."

Tristram drew his forearm roughly across his face, muttering to himself, so that Fleur could not quite hear, "Of course! Of course!"

"You do—believe me?"

"Of course!"

And he cast the frightened woman so savage a look, she stared at him for a long uncomprehending moment . . . and then sank sideways in a dead faint, utterly silent, as if her spirit had been extinguished within her.

And minutes later, Zoe emerged.

———

"*She* sleeps. So that *I* may speak."

"Zoe—?"

Fleur's gleaming hair lay loosed in a spill over the arm of the couch, where Tristram had carried her; a pulse beat at her left temple, and in the shallow indentation at the base of her throat, where Tristram had unbuttoned her high, tight collar. His anger had drained from him at once; he was suffused with so powerful a sense of shame, he might have been a child again, scolded for some small infraction of his father's household rules.

" 'Woman is to be adored,'—*she* cannot forget."

"What do you mean?"

"Zoe means what Zoe says. Zoe can speak only the truth."

"But Fleur—"

"I am *Zoe.*"

"—my poor darling—"

"Zoe is not 'poor,' Zoe is free," she whispered. "It is *she* who is 'poor,' while imagining herself free."

"But now the monster is dead."

"*She* knows how; but does not know."

"What do you mean?"

"She will love you—in her way."

" 'In her way'—?"

"The way of—false honor."

" 'False honor'—?"

"The way of weakness, of subterfuge, of acid-chastity, of pretty deceit!"

The words issued hissing, and quite surprised Tristram with their vehemence.

He was kneeling close beside Fleur, or Zoe, as she lay in a posture of helplessness on the couch; one of his arms cradling her head, and his face so close to hers that his breath, pantingly exhaled, stirred the wisps and tendrils of hair at her temples. He felt as if he were dangerously close to fainting, himself; or to bursting; both contrite, and enormously excited, as he had not been since his first encounter with Zoe on Delancy Street. It seemed to him that he and

this woman—*this* woman, and not the other—had had a
secret understanding between them all along, to the exclu-
sion of the rest of the world.

"I have put her to sleep—so that we may be alone. It has
been so long."

"My darling Fleur—"

"I am Zoe. Your Zoe."

"*My* Zoe."

Tristram kissed her; kissed her parted lips, and parted
them further; felt the woman's hot, darting, astonishing
tongue; and feared he would not be able to contain himself.
But she slapped lightly at him, and drew back, framing his
face with her hands; saying in an admonishing tone, "But
we have much to talk of, you and me! 'Angus' and 'Zoe.' "

Stupidly Tristram said, "I am 'Angus.' "

"And I am 'Zoe.' "

"—She knows nothing of you?"

"And nothing, or very little, of *you.*"

"She suspects nothing?"

Zoe laughed loudly, letting her head fall back against the
arm of the couch; so that Tristram saw yet more forcibly the
tiny pulse beating in her throat, which he wanted very badly
to kiss. "—She suspects everything," Zoe said. "When it
suits her."

"But you—she—claims to love me."

"Ah she does, she does! She 'claims.' "

"And to want to marry me."

"To 'want.' "

As if her fingers moved of their own accord Zoe was
slowly, languidly, teasingly unbuttoning the remaining buttons of her blouse; revealing by degrees, to Tristram's
yearning gaze, a portion of the infamous tattooing—the
miniature eyes, iridescent-blue, -green, -purple, -black, of
the peacock's tail; and the serrated red-glisten of what appeared to be an Oriental dragon's tongue, which Tristram
had not remembered. He would have buried his face in her
breasts had she not seized his head again, gripping it with
both hands in mock-maternal admonishment. "This is not

the time!" she said. "The time is rapidly approaching for love, but—this is not the time."

Tristram said, in anguish, "When I adore you so? When I have proven—?"

In her singsong Zoe crooned: "*This*, here, is a bed not a bed, in a room not a room, with so many looking on: *this cannot be.*"

Tristram did not understand, and felt desire very like despair. "But she *will* marry me,—*you* will marry me—won't you?"

"One day! One hour! When the monster is finally buried! Soon!"

"But—when? I am dying to love you, Fleur—I mean Zoe—"

"Do not confuse us, or we will exact our revenge!"

"But I love you both—"

"Impossible!"

"*He* did not love you both?"

"*He! Him!* Surely not!" Zoe's nostrils widened in contempt. "He did not know either of us—which necessitated his doom."

"But how, Zoe, *did* he die? I had thought I'd killed him in the park, but—"

Zoe shut her eyes tight, smiling, rocking slowly from side to side. "*She* sleeps, and Zoe wakes; Zoe sleeps, and *she* wakes; but both may sleep at once; that others may wake."

"—I had thought I'd killed him in the park, in the tunnel, but it was the wrong man, it seems to have been an innocent man," Tristram said, "—while at the same time—it must have been nearly the same time—your husband *did* die, *was* stabbed to death, at home. But I did not do it, I would swear I did not do it—"

"Swear, swear: 'If done, for love; for love only.'"

"For love, yes—"

"For *her* love, or mine?"

This question Tristram could not answer. In despair he said, "Tell me, Zoe, if you can—"

"Zoe speaks only the truth!"

"—if you know—"

"Zoe speaks only the truth, that *she* may speak none!"

"—why does Fleur shrink from me, from even my touch? Why, when she claims to love me?"

" 'She'—! Why love 'she'!"

"But I can't live without her! I have given over my life to her, as you must know—"

"As others have done, to their doom!"

"But why does she shrink from me? And yet look upon me so tenderly, and insist that she loves me? And that—"

"She fears your masculine repugnance, seeing the creature as she is, and not as she wishes to appear," Zoe said, suddenly impassioned, "—so horribly, in her eyes, so irrevocably, *exposed.*" She had opened the pleated silk blouse so that her small softly-plump breasts were revealed, each cupped from beneath by richly colored hieroglyphic figures stitched into the flesh, surrounding even the taut nipples; a sight, a vision, even more mesmerizing than Tristram recalled. *Writ in a language that has long gone by. And none can read the text, not even I.* Zoe continued to speak, in her taunting singsong; but Tristram no longer heard. Had he felt some revulsion for Grunwald's work, earlier? Had his flesh subtly crawled, exposed to the mutilated female body? Ah, how differently he felt now! "Beautiful," he whispered, staring. "No one so beautiful." He would have torn Zoe's clothes from her but she caught him up short, gripping his hair. He said, in a choked voice, "I want to save you!"

"You *have* saved me—at the cost of your own skin."

She then drew his head to her; cradled him hard and snug in her arms; and, for he knew not how long, Tristram lost himself in very bliss, in the madness of bliss . . . kissing, and tonguing, and sucking . . . grinding his face against the woman's perfumy body. Did he imagine it, or was he able to taste the slightly acetous dye of the "charm" . . . ?

4 And so Fleur Grunwald eluded him: and he never saw her again.

Or, if he saw her, it was at such a distance, and he was in so despairing a state, he could not have sworn it *was* her.

Repeatedly he telephoned the Delancy Street number, and repeatedly he was told she was not there; would not be there; had moved out; had moved away; and if he did not cease these calls the police would be notified, and— But at this point Tristram would have slammed down the receiver. "Someone is lying," he said aloud, his heart beating angrily, "—but surely it would not be *her.*"

Surely not? Not Fleur? Who had promised to marry him? Who had insisted she loved him? Who had sworn "eternal gratitude" to him? It was impossible to believe, thus Tristram did not believe it.

"She is newly widowed, and must be cautious," he concluded. "She is biding her time and I must bide my time too."

Though he did not much like the pronounced silvery streaks in his hair, shading, at the crown of his head, virtually into white: When had *this* occurred? And why? —And when he neglected to shave twice daily (as, of late, out of forgetfulness, was sometimes the case) his stubbled beard glinted a queer metallic white; giving Tristram, for all his attractiveness, and the cut of his clothes, a look as of one of the city's homeless wanderers: dishevelled, vagrant, slightly mad, and perhaps (if only slightly) dangerous.

And days passed. And days.

Though it was ludicrously expensive, and the hotel staff was just perceptibly less attentive than formerly, Tristram retained his suite in the Hotel Moreau. For Fleur had no other address or telephone number for the man she knew as "Angus Markham," should she wish to contact him.

Otto Grunwald's funeral was held in stately Episcopal splendor, attended by hundreds of mourners (as the newspapers repectfully noted): but Tristram Heade was not among them. Wisely, he kept his distance though a strong, very nearly sexual desire urged him to go . . . so that he might catch a glimpse of dear Fleur and perhaps even exchange a few words with her. "And also I might gloat a bit over the fact of the corpse," Tristram said thoughtfully, "—the monster now safely *dead*. For there is pleasure in justice, after all." But in the end of course he did not go to Grunwald's funeral.

Markham might have whispered in his ear that plainclothes detectives would attend the funeral, observing mourners closely. There would be secret photos taken, video films made. And Grunwald's nephew, Hans, had glimpsed Tristram's face that evening. . . .

So Tristram stayed away from the Grunwalds. Bided his time. Began to make small bets on horse races at the off-track betting—at first impulsively, then more methodically. (To his surprise and delight, he won most of his bets.) He read all he could discover of Otto Grunwald's unsolved murder and watched local television news avidly. *Shocking, tragic . . . vicious crime . . . well-known, much-admired Philadelphia philanthropist . . . unknown assailant sought.* Philadelphia police were particularly baffled by the fact that, on the night of the break-in, the burglar alarm system in Grunwald's mansion would seem to have been turned off.

"That," thought Tristram Heade, with a small, perplexed smile, "*is* strange."

But what of *his* crimes? Tristram objected. So many columns of newsprint, so much valuable television time, given over to eulogistic fantasies of Otto Grunwald's philanthropy:

and not a word, not so much as a hint, of the brute's perverse lusts . . . of the innermost workings of his soul. Tristram was seriously tempted to send the *Philadelphia Inquirer* a document listing Grunwald's crimes against Fleur, and against his previous wives; and, by extension, against all humanity. "Of course I would pay to have it typed," he shrewdly reasoned. "I would not write it in my own hand."

And the days passed.

And the fact of Poins's death dropped out of sight, seemingly forever; as if, in contrast to Grunwald's, it were of no worth. For this murder Tristram felt, at times, the nudging of conscience . . . and wondered if he should turn himself in . . . with an explanation of what he had done, and why; and how he was, in the deepest sense, innocent . . . though also guilty.

He decided not to act, however, until he next spoke with Fleur; for his responsibility, as lover and husband-to-be, was with her; and not elsewhere. It tore his heart to think that, if he were arrested for the death of a homeless vagrant, a man he had not, ah, he had not! meant to kill, his and Fleur's happiness would be forever ruined.

"Still, I am damned sorry for what I did," he told himself a dozen times a day, "—and really do wish, if it were possible, the harmless old crank might live again."

And one morning (it seemed by this time to be deeply spring, judging by the warmth, the fragrance of the air, the tulip-bordered green of Rittenhouse Square) two very mysterious things occurred.

First, Tristram read in the *Inquirer* the astonishing news that Philadelphia police had finally made an arrest in the Grunwald case; and that their suspect, a thirty-five-year-old black man, previously convicted of burglary, assault with a deadly weapon, violation of parole, etc., answered to descriptions of "suspicious loiterers" in the Burlingham Boulevard area; had no alibi for the night of Grunwald's death; and was known to have owned a hat very like, or identical with, the hat found on the ground beneath the forced window . . . a hat so idiosyncratic in style, police withheld all mention of it publicly, confident that, in time, as they proceeded with their investigation, it would be traced back to the killer. And so it was: or so it seemed.

The hat in the photograph was not Tristram's hat.

It was not a beret at all, but a cap, plaid, of the kind that British workingmen are commonly portrayed as wearing; its band covered with ornamentation of some kind, buttons, or decals; the hat "long associated" with Rufus S. Smith, the suspect, whose South Philadelphia neighbors identified it. And forensic experts were certain that . . . and Smith could not account for his whereabouts . . . and the pattern of his previous convictions suggested. . . . "But it is not my hat," Tristram exclaimed, clutching at his head. "They are arresting the wrong man."

He was sitting on the edge of his much-rumpled bed, smoking the remains of an ill-smelling cigar, unshowered, unshaven, clad only in silk underwear—the crotch uncomfortably tight, and the floral-patterned fabric painful to the eye: but Tristram's own more modest underwear had long since been used up, and he had procrastinated sending out his laundry—and he continued to sit there for a very long time, reading, and rereading, and again rereading the utterly puzzling article in the *Inquirer*. Had he known nothing of the circumstances of Grunwald's death he would certainly have thought, as the police did, that they had found their murderer; he would have done no more than glance at the photograph of the "incriminating" cap; he would have forgotten Rufus S. Smith's name immediately, and gone on to other news items. As it was, he sat befuddled; slack-jawed; rather sick at heart. Poor Rufus S. Smith! And poor Dr. Poins! It seemed to him a vicious thing, that Fleur's and his future happiness should depend upon the tragedies of, thus far, two utterly innocent victims. . . .

"And perhaps there will be more," he murmured, tapping thick gray cigar ash into the remains of a glass of scotch.

But the second development of that morning was even more astounding.

Midway in his breakfast (which continued to be fairly lavish, despite the malaise of recent days), Tristram was interrupted by a knock at the door; went to answer it with a sense of apprehension; and was handed a plain-wrapped package by the captain of the bellboys, who said it had been left downstairs at the desk. ANGUS MARKHAM and SPECIAL HANDLING REQUESTED were inked on it in neat block letters. Though sensing that he would have been happier had he not opened the door, Tristram tipped the man generously, and sent him away.

And what was inside the package but the black beret. . . .

With trembling fingers Tristram lifted it out. There was no note included. "What is this? *Why* is this? *Who is doing these things?*" For a long moment he stood unmoving, as if paralyzed; then went to a mirror and fitted the beret to his head; and it seemed to him unmistakable that it *was* the very beret (though now soiled and battered-looking) he had bought that morning at the Hotel Meridian. His reflection in the mirror showed a sallow-skinned, unshaven, rather dazed man, no longer young, though by no means old; a man with vague squinting pouched eyes, and a damp, slack mouth, and that silvery-white stubble Tristram so disliked.

He could have sworn he had already shaved, that morning.

5 *It is as if I, and by extension, my darling, you, are at the eye of a whirlwind, and cannot see the whirlwind; even to know it* is *a whirlwind. If you love me speak with me at once!*

—This risky telegram Tristram sent to *Mrs. Fleur Grunwald* at the Burlingham Boulevard address; but though he waited close by the telephone in his room for the remainder of the day, and for several days following, Fleur did not call.

The telegram was dated June 1.

6 *I am drowning in the mystery of your Absence; and of your (hypothetical) cruelty. You must know that I adore you (I continue to adore you) for have I not proven it? If you love me speak with me at once!*

—This yet riskier telegram Tristram sent; and again Fleur did not reply. The date was now June 19.

7

Yet Tristram reasoned that nothing could have happened to Fleur, since it would have found its way into print. As Otto Grunwald's widow, thus one of the wealthier members of Philadelphia society, she was surely the object of much public scrutiny. If she had left the city, if, for instance, she had had a breakdown of some kind, and had checked into a local hospital . . . it would have been reported, wouldn't it? Daily, Tristram scanned the society and gossip columns of the papers, nervously alert to any mention of *Grunwald*. But when his eye did pick up *Grunwald* the reference was never to Fleur.

Now when he telephoned the Delancy Street number a recording clicked hatefully on, informing him that the number had been changed; and that the new number was "not listed" in the directory. When he went to the house itself, and rang the buzzer, and knocked on the door, and even, once or twice, tried to peer into the ground-floor windows, it seemed quite clear that no one was home. (Can the earth have opened up to swallow them all? Tristram despaired.)

At last, though instinct seemed to be urging him strongly against it—a superstitious dread, perhaps, of returning to the scene of the crime—Tristram dared take a taxi to Burlingham Boulevard; asking to be let out a few blocks from the Grunwald estate, so that he could walk, presumably unobserved, the rest of the way. He had fortified his shaky nerves with a stiff shot of scotch, and had taken care to costume himself in quite ordinary clothes (his own, that is, and not Angus Markham's), but still he felt extremely ill at ease; *as if he were risking not only arrest, but another sort of catastrophe.* But I have no choice except to go forward, he thought. The woman I love has left me no recourse.

As Tristram approached the vicinity of the Grunwald estate he began to feel a visceral dread very like nausea. The neighborhood seemed emptied out, deserted—hardly any traffic along the boulevard, and no other pedestrians at all. A wan late-afternoon light, sepia in tone, rather grainy in texture, emanated from the aged plane trees that lined the street, and lifted from the parched grass edging the walks. Why, though it could not be more than mid-summer, was there a smell of leaves in the air, a taste of something gritty and autumnal . . . ? Tristram stood at the padlocked front gate of the entrance to Grunwald's house, and peered, with wavering vision, at the dun-colored mansion atop its small crest of a hill: how old it looked, and how distant, like a memory dimly recalled. The last glimpse Tristram had had of this house had been by night, and now too it seemed to possess a nocturnal quality, as in a color photograph taken at night; the camera's explosive flash having overcome the surrounding darkness—but only for a flash.

The once meticulously trimmed lawn was now overgrown with weeds, and queerly chopped-looking; the asphalt drive was marred by a thousand spidery cracks; a FOR SALE sign in vulgar red letters tilted in the grass. It seemed self-evident that the late Otto Grunwald's house was not only empty of all inhabitants but had been empty for a very long time. "Hello? Hello?" Tristram shouted. His fists closed on the iron bars of the gate until his knuckles grew white, and whiter still.

And how long he remained there, lost in thought, immobile, a tall, big-boned, rather slope-shouldered figure, head erect but with a look of profound bemusement, like an ox stunned by a sledgehammer blow, he could not have said. And what were the thoughts that careened through his brain, he could not have said.

It was after he had turned defeatedly away, and began walking a vague weaving southerly course back in the direction of the city, that he chanced to see the automobile as it sped past: saw it, at first, with no comprehension: a funereal-black but richly gleaming Rolls-Royce convertible, its top down, carrying a pair of young lovers (the man behind the wheel, the young woman snug beside him with her head resting on his shoulder) in the same direction in which he was headed. The elegant car eased past him soundlessly, and, emitting a trail of exhaust he could not see but could certainly smell, eased into the distance, as he stared. The most lethal poisons are invisible, Tristram thought.

He continued to walk, his pulse unhurried, though the taunting afterimage of the lovers burned in his vision: the high-held arrogant head of Hans Grunwald, and the lovely tousle-haired head of little Fleur.

V

1 *The mystery is too great for me. Too cruel.*

As the days began inexorably to lengthen, the season declining to autumn, Tristram's memory too began to shorten; rather, to shatter, like fragile crystal or ice, into fragments he could not (had he wished to do so) reassemble. He understood that a knowledge of reality—of that Reality that underlies mere surface scintillation and distraction—is dependent upon a close observation of facts; a grasp of how point A leads to point B, thus to C, D, E . . . and the rest. Not only the grasp of those secrets guiding human action, but the Secret guiding all secrets! He could not doubt (with all that remained in his veins of his highbred Virginia blood) that there is, finally, a meaning and a validity to the chaos of human experience; but this vision was not to be granted to him.

Nor, it began to seem embarrassingly clear, to "Angus Markham."

Tristram had long since settled his exorbitant bill at the Hotel Moreau, parting from that company with a good deal of bitterness ($1485 for room service deliveries alone!); and moving, with shrewd bachelor practicality, to a single room in a rooming house on Twenty-ninth Street near Drexel— a heterogeneous neighborhood of cheap hotels and rooming houses, taverns, pizza parlors, bowling alleys, all-night laundries. He had left no forwarding address behind, and he had informed no one back in Richmond of his whereabouts. The morbid intensity with which his thoughts focused upon *she-who-has-betrayed-me* (never again would he utter the cruel woman's name!) drained other subjects of significance, as a strong image in the foreground of a photograph weakens all the rest. But there were, now and then, bleak sunless mornings after whiskey-dazed but insomniac nights when Tristram found himself suddenly recalling, with pangs of old conscience, like old, outgrown clothes, the derelict in the tunnel (ah, what was his name?) he had so savagely stabbed, mistaking him for *her* husband . . . and the luckless black man (and *his* name? something like Smith? Jones? Brown?) who had been arrested, and by now, perhaps, even convicted, for a crime he had not committed. There is no hope for me if I do not turn myself in to the police, Tristram thought.

You will do nothing of the kind, fool.

But I have committed enormities!—I have destroyed human lives!

And so?

I have become a murderer *to no purpose.*

And so?

So Tristram vowed to confess to police, countless times; and within the hour forgot; his thoughts drawn remorselessly and bitterly to *she-who-has-betrayed-me.* Though one day, fortified by whiskey, and cleanly, if shakily, shaven, Tristram was indeed headed in the direction of the nearest police station when his eye chanced upon a racetrack form lying in the gutter . . . which he could not resist snatching up, and greedily reading. And then, all else forgotten, he decided to go to the nearest off-track betting parlor instead.

Another time, and this time having remembered to bring the murder weapon with him, Tristram was about to climb the steps to the precinct station when he had the uncanny sensation that he was being followed. The very hairs stirred at the nape of his neck, and he felt, in an instant, a primitive yet voluptuous fear. . . . When he turned he saw a man across the street, watching him; but looking quickly away when Tristram looked at *him*; a tall, thin, sunken-cheeked individual who wore a pale brown fedora low over his forehead, and a gabardine suit of so undistinguished a color and cut as to constitute virtual camouflage, and carried a folded newspaper under his arm. Tristram realized he had been seeing this man intermittently for the past several days. . . . A plainclothes detective, he thought. Panic gripped him. And though an instant before he had intended to confess to the crime of murder, and throw himself on the mercy of the state, he now trembled with fear. They will never catch me! he thought.

So he turned, and walked as swiftly as he dared, trying to maintain what he believed to be an air of urban casualness; entered a Florsheim's shoe store up the block, and blindly passed through it, and out a rear exit; now running along a litter-filled alley, his heart beating in his mouth; emerging at a busy street, and threading his way through traffic amid a din of horns and angry shouts; entering now another store, a record store, its aisles congested with young people and its very air quavering with deafening rock music; thwarted, for several agonizing seconds, from leaving that store by its rear exit, which seemed to have been barred over . . . in defiance, surely, of city fire laws? At last Tristram talked the manager into opening it for him, but not before the man in the fedora appeared in the doorway of the front entrance. . . .

Now perspiring and badly short of breath, Tristram ran down the alley behind the record store; emerged at another busy street, and crossed it; had the inspiration to hide in a movie theater, and went to buy a ticket (there was no line: the movie had begun a half-hour before), making an effort to be polite to the maddeningly slow and rather coquettish young woman who took his money. "You're sure in a hurry, mister," she said, amused, "—for somebody who's already late." "I'm not in a hurry!" Tristram said, pawing at the ticket she slid toward him.

Inside, Tristram saw to his distress that the theater was nearly empty.

He hurried down the aisle, however, and took a seat in a row occupied by two other solitary men—one of whom glanced up hopefully as he approached; close by an exit;

quite near the front. There he slouched in his seat, his gaze turned upward to the enormous screen, across which careened images he made no attempt to recognize, all his concentration focused elsewhere. Had he eluded the man? Surely he had eluded him? —But who *was* the man? And had he the power to arrest Tristram Heade, to dare to lock handcuffs on him, to lead him away, trapped and humbled like an animal on its way to slaughter, before the stares of idle strangers . . . ? They will never take me alive, he thought.

And at that moment he saw, in the corner of his eye, a man's figure appear in silhouette at the rear of the theater; the fedora hat still on, but the prop of the newspaper discarded. Tristram slouched further in his seat. He forced himself to stare up at the screen, though knowing that its kaleidoscope of rapidly shifting colors cast an unfortunate light upon his upturned face, which his canny pursuer could not fail to note. The man was starting down the aisle in Tristram's direction with deceptive casualness, and, unable to bear it any longer, Tristram bolted, making little effort to disguise his haste as he threw himself, hunched, head lowered, through a pair of long beaded curtains . . . ran along a close-smelling little corridor . . . shoved open the exit door, and stepped out into the alley. (It now appeared to be early evening: unless the overcast day had strangely darkened.) He reasoned that it would be futile to continue to run, and that the wisest strategy might be to confront his pursuer, and acknowledge his identity; if the man were a police detective, that could not be helped; and after all (as he tried to console himself) he had intended to turn himself in that day . . . hadn't he?

But when his pursuer stepped out into the alley, however, Tristram at once slipped a forearm around his neck, and, before knowing what he did, Markham's dagger being suddenly in his hand, he brought the sharp blade against the man's throat; and sliced, and sawed, and hacked away at it, with a ferocious strength that seemed to well up in him out of nowhere. And within seconds his pursuer, now his prey, lay vanquished at his feet, virtually gushing blood.

"My God! Again . . ."

It was not until later that evening, when, returned to the seclusion of his room, the door not only bolted but an armchair stolidly braced against it, that Tristram learned, to his astonishment, the identity of the man he had killed . . . in fact a detective, as Tristram had suspected; but not a detective with the Philadelphia police. Looking through the dead man's wallet, which he had had the presence of mind to take before fleeing, Tristram discovered that he was, or had been, a private investigator; he had a license issued by the Commonwealth of Pennsylvania, and a gun permit issued by the city of Philadelphia; and that his name (by the sheerest coincidence perhaps?) was Barton Joseph Handelman. And a carelessly folded carbon copy of a receipt, alleging the payment, only a few days before, of a $1400 retainer, yielded the information that Handelman's employer worked for a private investigation agency called Ajax Investigative Service . . . and that his employer was Morris Heade. Great-Uncle Morris Heade, with whom Tristram had not spoken in a very long time.

2

Following this episode, which upset him greatly at the time, Tristram began to sink, by degrees, into a disconsolate mood; his thoughts shifting obsessively from *she-who-has-betrayed-me* to *those-whom-I-have-injured*, and back again, with hellish repetition. Though most nights he made an effort to drink himself into oblivion he slept only fitfully: his room's single window opened out onto an air-shaft by way of which his nostrils were assailed by ripe, fruity, rancid odors rising from below, and he could hear indistinct voices punctuated by jeering laughter; if, maddened, he shut the window tight, and stuffed strips of Markham's silk handkerchiefs into his ears, the lumpy mattress kept him awake, with a sensation of things crawling . . . lice? bedbugs? roaches? Several times, believing himself awake, Tristram woke screaming from hideous nightmares, and caused such a commotion that his neighbors in the rooming house pounded on the walls and ceiling, and shouted threats. And sometimes, provoked beyond endurance by what he considered an invasion of his privacy, he gave vent to sheer rage, pounding violently back, and shouting, "Leave me alone! Murderers! I am an innocent man! Leave me alone—*or I'll kill you too!*"

With the consequence—and Tristram did not blame the man in the slightest—that his beleaguered landlord asked him timidly but firmly to move.

And so he moved, to another rooming house; then to a hotel near the railway station; gathering up his and Markham's commingled possessions, including the artificial eye, and the indelibly stained dagger, in his various suitcases. Had he been asked why he chose to remain in Philadelphia, and why, since he had a fair amount of money (including cash, from lucky bets on the races), he chose to live in such squalid and dispiriting surroundings, after the grandeur of the Hotel Moreau, he could not have said; except that conscience bound him to the city, and a sense of profound injustice—the injustice committed against him, and that which he himself had committed.

Increasingly too Tristram was prey to lascivious, shameful dreams, which flitted across his vision while he was fully conscious, and often in public places; nightmares in which the woman who had betrayed him and her naked, tattooed, writhing self were one. How she smiled at him with her moist lips, how boldly her arms coiled around his neck . . . ! If only, ah! that morning she had come to his hotel room! daring to take his hand in hers, and thanking him! declaring her love for him! declaring her eternal gratitude to him! and fainting, at his feet! alone in his room! allowing herself to be lifted in his arms! carried lifeless to a couch! if only, that morning! that hour! *that moment might be relived . . . !* Tristram's face burned and his eyes spilled over with tears; he was wretched with desire. Yet grateful that the woman was nowhere near, for fear of what, in male sexual rampage, he might do to her.

One evening he woke from an ugly dream of sinuous limbs, writhing loins, and sucking lips, to find himself walking in an unknown part of the city; his clothes dishevelled, and his hair blowing in his face. In sudden apprehension that, at last, he was losing his mind, and that Markham, for all his cold-bloodedness, was losing his mind too, Tristram located a tavern, and hurriedly ordered two shot glasses of whiskey, drinking both down, and then ordering a third . . . until his feverish brain cleared and he felt, to a degree, himself again. The tavern was a warm, rowdy, convivial place, the bar crowded with working-class men of diverse ages, and a scattering of women. How he envied their camaraderie—the evident simplicity of their lives! If they perceived Mystery in the world they were neither hypnotized nor defeated by it.

Is it too late for me to join them? *—It is.*

Close by Tristram's elbow lay pages of a discarded tabloid newspaper, which, out of habit, he could not help scanning. And, to his chagrin, saw, in the society section, *her* photograph, taking up half a page; hers, and the brute Hans's; the attractive young couple in evening dress at the opening of *Tristan and Isolde,* a benefit performance for the Multiple Sclerosis Society. . . . Otto Grunwald's widow wore an elegantly unadorned evening dress, black, long-sleeved, high-collared, with a single strand of pearls around her lovely throat, and her hair simply but very prettily arranged; and tall, husky, handsome Hans ("Mrs. Grunwald's frequent companion since the tragic death of her husband last April") wore a tuxedo whose cut seemed to emphasize the breadth and density of his shoulders. Tristram adjusted his glasses, and stared. There! there they were! openly! blatantly! defiantly! *so very obviously!*

In a paroxysm of rage he closed his fist in the page and threw it crumpled to the floor. And rushed out of the tavern without having paid for his third drink.

He saw it now, in its jeering crystal-clarity: how "Angus Markham" had been approached by the devious young wife, and seduced into killing her husband for her. *For her and her lover.* When the plot went awry, as a consequence of "Markham's" sudden cowardice, the lover himself, evidently waiting in the wings, had stepped in to complete it. Perhaps at first "Angus Markham" was to have been the dupe whom police would arrest and charge with the murder; then, having reconsidered, for what reason Tristram would never know, Hans tampered with the evidence, substituting one hat for another, one incriminating "clue" for another. . . . How cleverly the scheme had been contrived, yet how naturally it had seemed to unfold, so that Tristram Heade, or "Angus Markham," manipulated at every turn, had imagined *he was guiding the scheme himself.*

"And shall I ever revenge myself upon them? Shall I ever

redress the balance? —No: there have been too many killings already."

And he seemed to know too that he would never again
be in a position to so much as approach the lovers; in their
youth, their beauty, their newly acquired wealth, their very
guilt,—which surely bonded them as deeply as others are
bonded by mere innocence—they had ascended to another
dimension of being to which, in *his* state, he had no access.
Neither he, nor "Angus Markham."

For hours that night Tristram walked, walked . . . hoping to
lose himself in the outward world, as, it seemed, he had so
hopelessly lost himself in the inner. What has propelled me
to *this* moment, *this* seemingly so vagrant point in time? Is
it fate, or mere chance? But is chance "mere"? *Is chance
fate?* His trajectory, blind as it was, and fueled by passion
and despair, nonetheless led him in what must have been a
large looping circle; so that, near dawn, he found himself
inhaling the ashy garbagey odor of a familiar place . . . the
Chancellor Street mews in which Lux's Rare Books & Coins
was located. A sudden impulse, buoyed by a sensation very
like happiness (which Tristram had not felt for some time),
led him to the shop; and he began knocking on the door
before he realized it was perhaps too early for such a visit
. . . and before his senses quite took in the fact that Lux's
antiquarian establishment had been taken over by a taxi-
dermist. He had been thinking that he might simply turn
back the clock; begin again, as if it were the second day of
his Philadelphia visit; making, in a sort of Adam-like innocence, the purchase of that suspect quarto edition of *Macbeth* Lux had been urging upon him, and Tristram had
spurned as a fake. . . . But of course this was not to be: in
the cramped shop window were, now, not books, but
stuffed creatures, each affixed to its pedestal or perch, yet
sadly crowded together, like a menagerie in some tight-
encompassed airless space (like Hell); a squirrel with an
erect, bushy tail; a hare whose widened eyes were the very
mirrors of terror; an owl whose flattened face, tawny eyes,

and smooth-brushed feathers quite pierced Tristram's heart, reminding him of . . . he knew not what; a spider monkey halted in the act of climbing a chunk of tree, small intelligent wizened face cramped over its shoulder, slender tail turned upward in a question mark. . . . "Poor things! Who has done this horror to you!"

Tristram was about to turn away in despair when the door was noisily unbolted and opened by a white-haired little man who glared up at him angrily. "Yes? What? Who is it? At this hour of the morning?" The man wore rubber gloves, and a harsh chemical odor lifted from them, stinging Tristram's eyes.

After a few minutes' exchange it developed that Virgil Lux had died suddenly, and his stock had been sold at auction. Tristram expressed shock, for he had not heard. He had badly wanted, he said, to buy a book . . . a certain priceless book Lux had been holding for him. "Too late," the little man said, screwing up an eye at Tristram, "—too late, son, they did him in. In this very shop, at the rear. As they are doing us all in, one by one." " 'They'—? Who do you mean?" Tristram asked. "Or maybe it was only one of 'em, a burglar, or a robber," the little man said with a careless shrug, "—or one of these young kids all hopped up with drugs. In any case they got him, and he's gone. And *I'm* here. *And I mean to stay.*" This last was uttered with an air of belligerence; Tristram, by instinct, took a step back. He was still so very surprised, rather stunned . . . poor Virgil Lux! . . . Dead, buried, gone, his life's work erased as if it had never been, and his meticulously acquired stock scattered to the four winds! In that instant, in contemplation of the tragedy that yet seemed, like all our private tragedies, merely an event, a ripple or shudder of a sort in the fluid flow of the quotidian, Tristram quite forgot his suspicion of the man, and his grudge against him. "How did Mr. Lux die? How, I mean, did they kill him?" Tristram asked. " 'Multiple stab wounds,' is what I heard, and the murder never solved," the old man said, again screwing up an eye at Tristram, "—and the police prob'ly not giving a good

God damn, you know, but just let it ride, and turnin' 'em loose on the street if they do catch 'em, all I know is what I read in the paper, myself, 'cause nobody around here much wants to talk about it, like there's a kind of dread in the air, some sickness you can almost smell, y'know, if one of us's struck down and we maybe don't see it maybe it won't happen to us too, like, you might know, the mentality of the deer,—you ever go deer hunting, son?—one of 'em shot down and falls, and the others sometimes don't take no notice, just keep on browsing, keep their heads down, that's the mentality of certain deer and that's the mentality of a lot of people these days, but, yes, son, all I know is my predecessor *did* die, they stabbed the poor old son-of-a-gun to death, and left a bloodstain on the floor nobody could ever scour out, and I got covered with some linoleum, and that's, y'know, that.'' And he broke off his long brisk speech and shut the door and left Tristram standing in the alley, staring thoughtfully into mere space.

3 "What is it? Who? Is someone there . . . ?"

Frequently, he woke in the night with the sudden conviction that someone *or something* was watching as he slept; his teeth chattering with fear, and a sickly cold perspiration coating his body. For long minutes he lay paralyzed; his life passing rapidly before his eyes, like a landscape seen from a speeding train; he seemed to sense that his life—his life as *he* had known it—was coming to a close, and what was to be done? He was a murderer, and lacked the courage to confess to his crimes.

(How ashamed his father and mother would be, if they knew! But Tristram could barely remember them by now. There were times, to be quite frank, when he could not remember them at all. Did they die before I was born? he wondered.)

It was Otto Grunwald's artificial eye that watched him, thus there was nothing for Tristram to do, to quell his fright, but to switch on the light, and check . . . the utterly lifeless, synthetic object . . . mere *plastic* lying in a cheap ashtray atop the dresser . . . possessed nonetheless of a malevolent interior radiance, and the ability to see. Tristram stared at the thing, and the thing seemed to stare back. Assuming that the artificial eye was a perfect mate of Grunwald's real eye, this was also, in a sense, Grunwald's "real" eye too . . . the iris a pale, anemic brown, flecked with hazel; the "white" a stained-ivory hue, so subtly permeated with tiny blood capillaries that Tristram had to put on his glasses, and peer very closely, before he could make them out. Though the eye appeared just perceptibly to have grown larger there were no other changes in it, so far as Tristram could make out; it never moved from its place in the ashtray; and of course it *was* dead, it *was* blind . . . wasn't it?

Tristram wondered if Grunwald had been buried with one eyeless socket, or whether the cosmetician who had prepared the corpse had supplied it with a substitute. Or, since the dead man's eyes would be closed in any case, perhaps it would not matter? Tristram had located nothing in any of the newspapers about Grunwald's missing eye; another bit of information shrewdly withheld by police, he supposed. For only the killer would have the eye. The proof of the killer being that he had the eye.

And here in Tristram Heade's room (on the third floor, rear, of the Camelot Hotel) *was* the eye; the incriminating eye; but no one knew, and no one seemed to care.

Precisely how Tristram spent his days, apart from sporadic visits to betting parlors in the city, and long intense yet inconclusive afternoons at the public library (he was compiling a list of "Womankind's Offenses Against Man"), and desultory meals in bar-restaurants, and episodes of drinking which left him amnesiac, it would be difficult to say; as our days, passing, in a bright yeasty stream of individual moments, like pulse beats, seem always on the verge of defining themselves, yet never do. How many months had it been since the shock of reading of Otto Grunwald's death in the newspaper?—since the yet more profound shock of *her* betrayal? The refrain sounded obsessively in Tristram's head, *An eye without a confining socket is a terrible thing to behold.*

The Camelot Hotel, where chance had brought Tristram, was an aged building close by the railway station, of no architectural distinction; permeated by the odors of decades, and, at all hours of the day or night, promiscuous noises, which sometimes set Tristram's sensitive nerves on edge but more often provided a strange sort of comfort, for this was a veritable haven of anonymity, in which Tristram's noises, should he wish to make any, would not be heard. Indeed,

when he was wakened from bad dreams by his own screaming and thrashing about, his neighbors to each side, and
above and below, rarely responded with angry thumps and
screams of their own; nor did the hotel manager chide him.
"The privacy of the grave," Tristram observed wryly, "—or
nearly."

And, though housekeeping services were said to be provided, no one ever entered Tristram's room, so far as he
knew.

So it was a considerable shock, when, returning to the hotel
from his visit to Chancellor Street, Tristram discovered that
the door to his room was unlocked; and had been left discreetly ajar by an inch or so, to inform him, as he approached, that it *was* unlocked, and that someone was
probably inside.

Swallowing hard, giving himself no time to speculate,
Tristram pushed the door boldly open, and there stood,
broadly smiling, hands on his hips, patently waiting for
him,—ah, what was his name: the detective Tristram had
hired months ago, and to whom he had paid a healthy retainer, to track down the whereabouts of Angus Markham.

This wiry little fellow looked precisely as Tristram remembered, except that he wore a boxy green-gray tweed suit, a
dark green shirt open at the collar, and his thinning hair
was slicked down more neatly atop his skull. The violet-
amber glasses were pushed primly against the bridge of his
nose; his cuff links glittered; he had heard Tristram's footsteps, and, in virtually the same instant Tristram opened the
door, his hand shot out with such ebullient swiftness that
Tristram was momentarily taken aback, not understanding
it was merely a *handshake* the detective offered. "Ah, Mr.
Heade! At last! Hel-*lo*! I found your door unlocked, or," and
here he smiled more winningly, and winked, "—or nearly.
So I hope you won't mind my inviting myself in, to wait for
your return? (And it has been a considerable wait, indeed,
Mr. Heade: you seem to have been gone the entire night.)
There is no lobby downstairs, and this is so *public* a place,

I'm afraid I would be recognized. And, of course, it has been many weeks since we've last laid eyes on—''

Tristram took in none of this. "Handelman," he said, staring. "Your name is—"

"Bud Handelman, of course," the detective said, squinting at Tristram as if he thought he might be joking. "In your employ!"

"Ajax Investigative—"

"*Achilles* Investigative Service," Handelman said quickly, with a quick look of pain, "—my brother worked for Ajax. No, I am *your* man, Mr. Heade, I am in *your* confidential employ. *Invincible and unbribable*—our firm's motto!"

"Your—brother?" Tristram said, staring.

"Who is not our concern here, Mr. Heade," Handelman said, blinking, and frowning, for an instant seemingly on the verge of tears, "—for *I* am your man, and I think you will be interested in my report, which I have completed at last; completed, that is, so far as I have been able." His smile, for an instant tremulous, now became quite dazzling. "You yourself were a tricky figure to 'track down'!" he said, wagging a forefinger. "I hope you had not given up on our little project? I hope you had not *forgotten*—?"

"Forgotten—?"

"That you empowered me to investigate the background and the whereabouts of an 'Angus Markham,' and to prepare a confidential report to you?"

Tristram murmured, "Oh, no, of course I have not forgotten. It's just that—the surprise of—"

"I know! I know! I apologize, Mr. Heade!" Handelman said cheerfully. In a brisk darting movement he slipped past Tristram's elbow to shut the door, and bolt it. "Now, we can waste no more time, and get down to business. As I said, I think you will be interested in—"

Handelman had taken up a large portfolio lying atop Tristram's bed, and, inviting Tristram to sit, as if this were his room, and Tristram a guest, began to read, "Confidential report submitted to T. Heade, client, by B. Handelman, licensed investigative agent, in the matter of—" The little man's bright chatter splashed over Tristram like a stream over a large inert rock in its path; yet, by degrees, Tristram regained enough presence of mind to assure himself that he was in no immediate danger; the intruder was not a police officer, but a man in his own employ; and all that passed between them was confidential. Even if Handelman had spied the artificial eye atop the dresser . . . even if he had had the audacity to do a search of Tristram's things, and had discovered the faintly bloodstained dagger between the mattress and the box springs of the bed . . .

Handelman seemed to be concluding a sort of prefatory section, to the effect that, though the exact whereabouts of Angus Markham were not known at the present time, and no actual sighting of the subject had occurred, a good deal of information had been gathered, to be placed at the disposal of the client. He glanced up at Tristram, squinting. "Mr. Heade? Shall I proceed? Or is this an inconvenient time? —Or am I reading too quickly?"

Tristram said quietly, as if his fate were now to be revealed, "Please proceed, Mr. Handelman. The time will never be more convenient."

4 By degrees there emerged a sordid but fascinating account, related in Handelman's boyish voice, of a warped, diabolically clever, doubtless psychopathic personality, only one of whose numerous aliases was "Angus T. Markham"; a man of between thirty-five and forty years of age, possibly a native of Florida, but known to speak with several regional accents (including Virginian); who seemed to have fashioned a career for himself of professional gambling, real estate speculation, "confidence games" of various shades of audacity, and,—and here Handelman paused for dramatic effect, casting a squinty glance at Tristram—the exploitation of wealthy women, usually widows.

"Which is to say, so far as police in five states have reason to suspect," Handelman said, "—*murder.*"

"Murder—!" Tristram's lips moved of their own accord.

Handelman shuffled his papers, one side of his babyish face crinkled in grudging admiration. "I must say I was impressed!" he chuckled. "Your 'Markham,' in whichever of his guises, has quite a record!—though not *officially*, I should make clear, since police have never actually arrested him, and, so far as I could discover, he has never stood trial in any state. I began my search in Tampa, following your lead, and showed the photograph around, and very soon had some luck, since there, it seems, under a pseudonym— a sort of anagrammatization: 'Mark A. Andrus'—he is wanted for questioning in the death of a widow by the name of—" and here Handelman shuffled his papers further, and pulled out a sheet to bring close to his eyes, "—'Martha

Klingerman,' formerly 'Mrs. Harold S. Klingerman,' fifty-two years old at the time of her death. A beautiful woman, I was informed, married to a much older man, a wealthy Tampa businessman, who died in a fall from the eighteenth floor of one of his own buildings in downtown Tampa, in July 1983 . . . following which, after two months, Mrs. Klingerman married a man named 'Mark A. Andrus' of whom little was known except that he seemed to make a living at the racetrack and was, according to friends of Mrs. Klingerman's, 'fantastically charming.' In marrying Andrus Mrs. Klingerman made the fatal error of totally revising her will in his favor, and signing over to him most of her assets, even granting him, for no reason anyone could discover, power of attorney; with the consequence that, after six months of marriage, the poor woman herself perished in an automobile accident believed 'suspicious' by the insurance company . . . though no evidence was ever brought forward of foul play, and the police investigation went nowhere, and no charges were brought against Andrus, who shortly disappeared from the area. Thus, Tampa! The trail led next to Sarasota, where, a year later, in early 1985, our elusive friend emerges, under the name 'Andrew S. Hammark,' involved this time in a real estate scheme of such ingenuity and complexity I don't believe I ever quite understood it; except, again, the wife of a wealthy businessman—this, one 'Eloise S. Farquhar,' thirty-eight-year-old wife of 'Ulysses Farquhar'—was befriended, wooed, and won; following which her husband died in a boating accident on the Gulf, and within two months she married Hammark, and, like the unhappy Mrs. Andrus in Tampa, revised her will in favor of her new husband, and signed over to him her assets, and granted him power of attorney; with results that should not surprise us. In September 1985 the former Mrs. Farquhar died, according to the coroner's report,"—Handelman rather dramatically brought a darkly photostated paper close to his eyes, "—of an overdose of a painkilling drug prescribed by her doctor. The coroner's jury ruled the death 'misadventure,' a polite term for suicide, and—and this, Mr. Heade, is a tribute to our friend's 'fantastical charm'!—not a single member of the deceased's family tried to bring charges against Hammark; who, like Andrus, shortly disappeared from the area. Isn't it remarkable? And next we arrive at—"

"Key West," Tristram said tonelessly.

"Indeed: Key West. Where, in December 1985, a very peculiar incident occurred, involving the disappearance of a forty-year-old man named 'Mason P. Hinkman,' a broker and real estate entrepreneur, and his reappearance after twelve days as, it seems, in retrospect, another man. That is, 'Hinkman' did disappear, was in fact thrown from a moving train,—the corpse was found months later, badly decomposed, at the foot of a railroad embankment in the country—but another 'Hinkman' seems to have taken his place, impersonating the man not only to his business partners and associates but *to his own wife and children.* How long the deception could have been sustained, one can't guess, but it did last long enough for our friend—and there is no doubt but that the murderer *was* our friend: photographs of Hinkman resembled the photograph of 'Markham' in my possession—to help himself to as much ready cash out of his victim's savings and assets as he could; and after a week or so he disappeared. 'Into thin air, for the second time,' as Mrs. Hinkman told me. Thus, Key West! Isn't it remarkable?"

Handelman glanced up smiling at Tristram, who was sitting very still, his hands tightly clasped on his lap, and his eyes, behind the slightly misted lenses of his glasses, penetratingly fixed to the other's face. "—Remarkable, I mean, in two ways," Handelman added, "—that the man you think of as 'Angus T. Markham' was so clever, and so cruel; and that his victims, his dupes, seem, at least to us, so very—" he shook his head in wonderment, grinning, "—*credulous.*"

Tristram's voice seemed to rise, with enormous effort, from someplace deep inside him. "The world is founded upon credulousness, Mr. Handelman. Credulity. It is another word for faith."

"Another word," Handelman said, with a dimpled laugh, "—for stupidity."

Tristram stared, and made no reply. From somewhere close by, on the street, came a sudden blare of sirens; which neither man seemed to hear.

Smiling, animated, his voice rising and falling with a childlike pleasure in performance, the detective returned to his elaborately prepared report; reading for nearly an hour; tracking his elusive subject to Palm Beach . . . to Baltimore . . . to Washington, D.C. . . . to Manhattan . . . to Pittsburgh . . . to Fredericksburg, Virginia, where, in March of this very year, he seemed to have dropped from sight. Tristram listened, and did not listen; heard, and did not hear; his glasses several times so befogged with condensation he had to remove them and polish them; his heart beating steadily, yet not hard; his head as empty as the not-yet-filled cylinders of a revolver. Once or twice a sigh escaped from him loud enough, or despairing enough, to cause Handelman to glance up, squinting, and to inquire, "Is this all too much for you, Mr. Heade? Would you like me to stop? Or to summarize the rest?" Tristram shook his head, no, not at all, too strangely fatigued to speak; but thinking, Neither of us is going to escape so easily.

In all, it seemed that "Angus T. Markham" was involved in a number of murders, possibly as many as eleven, in five states, within the past six years; primarily of women, but, in three probable instances, of men. The female victims were without exception the wives of older, fairly wealthy men; the eldest, Mrs. Klingerman, was fifty-two, and the youngest, a Baltimore heiress, was only twenty-seven; though varying considerably in temperament, education, and background, each of the women had a reputation as a local beauty, and was therefore attractive enough to seem to have warranted the legitimate romantic interest of the man known as "Angus T. Markham." ("There is even the possibility, which I throw out as mere speculation," Handelman said thoughtfully, "—that our murderous friend did fall in love with these women, one by one; and did adore them as he seems to have sworn he did; but immediately lost interest in them as soon as he married them, and they were 'his.' Perhaps, once they were 'his,' he came to loathe them? I have heard that such behavior characterizes the psychopathic personality.") By contrast, the male victims conformed to a fairly narrow model: each was between the ages of thirty-two and forty-two; each was comfortably well-to-do, though not spectacularly rich; and each resembled "Markham" to an astonishing degree, or "he" resembled him, since "he" was able to slip into his life and impersonate him without being detected. . . .

Tristram said softly, "Yes."

Handelman concluded by saying that the trail went cold the previous April, when "Markham" seemed to have boarded the train Tristram took, probably in Richmond, where Tristram boarded it; but seemed not to have arrived in Philadelphia. "Thus we come to the present time, or nearly," Handelman said, closing his portfolio with a snap, "—the subject's whereabouts, so far as Bud Handelman could discover, 'unknown.' I tried a number of leads but each proved worthless, as if the man had indeed disappeared into thin air! Or gone flying from that train into a bog! And I began to worry that you were losing patience, Mr. Heade, waiting so many weeks for a report; and might object to the expenses I was accumulating on the road. So I tried to contact *you,* and had some difficulty, at first, but, well, I persevered,—and here I am." His eyes were eerily magnified behind their thick lenses; his small, round, babyish face seemed lit from within, with innocent pride. Tristram thought, staring, *This man is my friend: my only friend.* Then, in the next instant, *This man cannot be allowed to live.*

Tristram removed his glasses, and rubbed vigorously at his eyes; as if, perhaps, he hoped to rub the vision out of them. With a wan smile he said, "But that is only the tip of the iceberg, I suppose? Eleven deaths? We know, don't we, —I mean, we can surmise—that a man like 'Markham,' depraved as he clearly seems, and insensible to the sufferings of others, would probably have killed many more?"

"It's quite possible," Handelman said, nodding brightly. "A serial murderer; a psychopath; very shrewd, very mercurial, very quick to adapt himself to changing circumstances—yes, it's quite possible, even probable, that he has, during the course of his lifetime, killed many more than eleven people. But my trail began in Tampa, in 1983. For a private investigator, a trail must begin somewhere, and it is sometimes arbitrary."

Handelman extracted from an inside pocket a much-folded sheet of paper, which, with a slightly shy gesture, he handed to Tristram. It was a minutely itemized expense account with such headings as "travel," "lodging," "meals," "telephone calls," and "incidentals." The last-named was particularly high, and, seeing Tristram's expression, Handelman said quickly, " 'Incidentals' includes payment to informers. What one might call bribes."

Tristram was holding the expense sheet in his hand, and seemed to be closely examining it; but said, after a moment, "Have you ever encountered anyone like 'Angus T. Markham' in your investigative work before?"

"Well—I didn't encounter 'Markham' in the flesh!" Handelman said with a boyish self-deprecatory laugh. Then, more seriously: "No, I must admit I have never had a case quite like this. I have done surveillance on two or three decidedly psychopathic personalities, but they were not actual murderers; still less were they serial murderers like our friend 'Markham.' " Handelman leaned brightly forward and said, with a confidential air, "Most of a private investigator's work, you know, is fairly routine; not at all as the popular media would have it. It can yield dangerous moments, of course, but it is more often monotonous; even clerical; the slow, patient, meticulous accumulation of facts, minutiae, 'evidence.' We investigators poke our noses about in the dustheap of the world to get information on such utterly commonplace men and women, it is astonishing to believe that anyone in his right mind would pay for such services! —But your 'Angus T. Markham' is a very different proposition altogether."

"And you never, so far as you know, caught a glimpse of him?"

"Ah no! Of course not!" Handelman said, opening his eyes wide. He smiled at Tristram as if suspecting him of a joke. "If I had, I would have included that in my report; I would have been very proud of *that*."

"And his current whereabouts are unknown?"

"Unknown to *me*!—to *us*! But not, after all, unknown to *him*."

"You think the man is still living?"

Handelman lowered his voice, and touched a forefinger lightly to his lips. "It is my hunch, wholly *ex tempore*, that, yes, the man is living, still. And will simply resurface, elsewhere, or has already done so, in another guise."

"And kill again?"

"If no one prevents him?—very likely yes."

Tristram seemed to consider this, his gaze downcast, and his nostrils widened in breathing; he had been sitting nearly motionless for some time, and now seemed to rouse himself, in quick nervous rippling little shivers. "You will want your payment," he said quietly. And yet he remained sitting, and made no move to get his checkbook from its hiding place in the lining of one of Markham's suitcases, piled with the other pieces of luggage in a corner of the room. A thought occurred to him. "May I have the photograph back?"

"Ah yes! Of course!" The detective drew the photograph out of an inside vest pocket, and handed it over to Tristram, murmuring apologetically, "I'm afraid it seems to have clouded a bit more, though I can't think why—I'm sure I didn't expose it unnecessarily to the sun."

Tristram did no more than glance at the familiar malevolent likeness, and, in an action that seemed to startle Handelman, tore the photograph into halves, quarters, and eighths, and let them fall where they would on the floor. He was breathing so deeply, though so calmly, his nostrils widened pronouncedly with the effort. "No more killings," he murmured.

Another thought occurred to him. "Have you been a

detective for very long, Mr. Handelman?'' he asked, with an effort at sociable warmth. "You seem quite young.''

Handelman blushed with pleasure, like a man to whom such direct questions are rarely put. He said, wryly, "I am perhaps not so young as I look!'' Then, more soberly: "In a sense I have been a detective all my life. I come from a family of detectives—that is, most of the men in my family, on my father's side, have been detectives. 'Private investigators.' My great-great-grandfather did some top-flight investigative work for Horace Greeley—you have heard of Horace Greeley?—the crusading editor of the New York *Tribune*, in the mid-1800s?—particularly in uncovering the secrets of the Ku Klux Klan; my great-grandfather was a top Pinkerton man, and led a small revolt of his fellows out of the agency when Henry Clay Frick—you have heard of Frick?—*not* an art museum, you know, but chairman of Carnegie Steel—hired Pinkerton's men by the hundreds to fight picketing workers, and fire upon defenseless men and women. And my grandfather, and my father—'' He blushed more deeply, and said, "But I must stop: I am boring you!''

"You are not boring me,'' Tristram said, "—you are not boring me at all.'' He paused; he saw that his hands were trembling, but so finely no one might see. He said, "I like you. I think you are a good, decent man, and I like you.'' He swallowed hard. "You are my only friend.''

How this peculiar statement struck the young detective, Tristram did not know; for he dared not look at the man's face, and said, quickly, "And in your own generation?—the Handelmans continue to be private investigators?''

"There are only two of us now,'' Handelman said, slowly, "—I mean, there were. My elder brother Barry died not long ago in the line of duty.''

"Died?''

"Was killed.''

"Ah, killed! I'm terribly sorry to hear it!'' Tristram exclaimed. "—But how did it happen? 'In the line of duty'—how?''

Handelman sat quietly, staring at the floor. An expression of childlike hurt, pain, and loss passed over his face; his small jaw hardened, in the instinct to resist tears. "I would rather not speak of it at this time," the detective said quietly. Then: "It has been said that 'The detective story is a tragedy with a happy ending,' but it is not so, always. In fact it is rarely so. Tragedy, yes; happy ending, no."

"Even if you 'get your man'?"

Handelman's moist gaze lifted to Tristram, with a look of patient irony. Though the detective could not have been more than twenty-seven or -eight years old that look bespoke decades of experience. He said softly, "It is always doubtful, Mr. Heade, whether a detective 'gets his man,' or 'his man gets him.' For evil triumphs, in the end."

"Evil? Triumphs? In the end? But why?—why do you say that with such conviction?" Tristram exclaimed, shocked.

For a moment it looked as if Handelman was about to speak; then, thinking better of it, he drew a large, not very clean handkerchief out of his pocket, and touched a corner to his eyes, each in turn; then rose, clearing his throat, with a gesture meaning it was time for him to leave—and time, perhaps, for him to be paid.

So Tristram too rose from his seat, slowly, rather clumsily, like a man in a dream.

As if loosed from their confinement words careened through his brain *There was the Door to which I found no Key There was the Veil through which I could not see* like freight cars rattling in the night, emerging out of nowhere and disappearing into nowhere *Some little talk awhile of Me and Thee There was—and then no more talk of Thee and Me* and, more urgently, *Taking yourself by surprise you take your quarry by surprise as well.* Breathing rather hard, he said, "Let me get my checkbook, Mr. Handelman! It's hidden between the bedsprings and the mattress,—excuse me just a moment!"

He bent, tugging at the mattress; a terrible roaring rose in his ears. The detective said, "May I help you, Mr. Heade?" But when he placed his child-sized hands next to Tristram's, the two men straining to lift the mattress, but having difficulty getting, at first, the proper leverage, Tristram gently nudged him away; and surprised both Handelman and himself by sitting down, hard, on the edge of the bed, as if, overcome by a sudden spell of dizziness, he had lost his balance. "I only now remembered," he said, embarrassed, "—my checkbook isn't here, but in one of my suitcases. Hidden in a secret compartment in one of my suitcases. There, over there, in the corner of the room— that big leather one."

Though it could hardly be said that Tristram was feeling altogether himself, and frank terror lurked at the edges of his consciousness, like a flood of darkness preparing to spill into a sunlit room, he accompanied the detective along the hotel corridor, and, the elevator being, as nearly always, not working, down several flights of grime-encrusted fire stairs, rife with the odors of disinfectant, vomit, and stale urine. He might have said he meant to protect the little man, in this questionable place; yet surely—and this was a thought he only now considered—Handelman carried a revolver? Strapped into a holster, discreetly hidden inside his over-sized greenish tweed coat? At the foot of the stairs the men shook hands another time, and Handelman, his face quite pink with pleasure, thanked Tristram another time, both for the promptness with which he had paid his bill, and his "unexpected generosity,"—for Tristram had pressed into Handelman's hand several hundred-dollar bills, in token, as he said, of his personal esteem. "You have eradicated all Mystery for me regarding this 'Markham,' and cleansed my soul," Tristram said passionately. "You have shown me the path I must now take: it is *I* who am grateful to *you*."

Handelman turned to leave, but Tristram detained him, with another thought—as if to hold at bay, if only for another few seconds, the flood of terror that awaited him. "The artificial eye in the ashtray on my dresser: you must have noticed it? You must have wondered what it was?" he asked, lightly. Handelman blushed even more, and smiled a boyish, rather guilty smile. "Oh no, I didn't wonder! Not at all!" Tristram said, "You weren't curious?—you didn't think the eye, well, an oddity, there, resting in my ashtray; an item sui generis; perhaps a 'clue'?" Rather pedantically, Handelman said, "There are no 'clues' apart from the specificity of cases, Mr. Heade. That is the first principle of detection. If I had wondered, unsolicited, about the eye on your bureau, which I assure you I did not, I would very likely have theorized, you know, that it was a personal memento of some kind; or a good luck charm; or, perhaps, a spare eye of your own—a spare artificial eye, I mean."

And, limping slightly, the little detective walked off, with Tristram staring in astonishment after him.

5 "And now it is all clear."

"And now I can no longer refuse to acknowledge the horror."

"That I myself am—*the horror.*"

For it was, now, absolutely and incontestably clear, that Tristram Heade no longer lived; and that the murderous psychopath Angus T. Markham had taken his place.

Except—not entirely. As a host-victim is taken over by a parasite, which, initially at least, is careful not to drain too much nourishment from him, wanting the host-victim to remain alive as long as possible. So there is a small part of "Tristram" that remains, Tristram thought. But how long, in the face of "Markham's" invasion, will he endure?

And so, it must end.

Tristram was standing before a spotted mirror, and began now vigorously to brush his hair with twin tortoiseshell brushes. His wire-rimmed scholar's eyeglasses winked slyly at him. He knew what he must do, and would: he must cross the room to the window *as if I were already dead.* "No more deaths by my—or his—hand. Ever again." He would touch the windowpane with cool, trembling fingers—he would press his forehead against it, his head prayerfully bowed— he would summon forth his deepest strength, and shut his eyes, and make the plunge—into oblivion. *And so absolve myself. Redeem my sins. Farewell, Tristram Heade!*

Except: a fleck of lint on his lapel caught Tristram's eye, and he brushed it irritably away. Even in death poor grooming would be inexcusable. And God knows he needed a fresh haircut and a shave—the bracing restorative shave that only a gentlemen's barber, in an exclusive European-style hotel, can provide. And—where was his eau de cologne Narcisse? He glanced about, frowning, his irritation rapidly mounting.

It was low blood sugar merely. He was ravenous with hunger, and very thirsty. Time to dine? What time *was* it? Too much thinking! conscience pricking! It got on a man's nerves! it did not amuse! A vision of lightly poached oysters topped with caviar shimmered before him, his mouth watered at the prospect of a fine crisp chardonnay. . . . Yes, but he would begin with a scotch on the rocks. It was that hour of the day, and more than that hour. Already he had turned from the window, the telephone receiver in his hand; already he had dialed a familiar number, and a cultured voice at the other end answered, "Le Bec Fin, how can we help you?"

"A table for one, 'Heade' the name, in twenty minutes—thank you."

An unhurried, meditative meal; an evening's rich, stimulating self-examination; a contemplation of possibilities for the future—in this way, Tristram had no doubt, the issue would be resolved.